Running From Sunday

Rene' Stanley

Books By Rene'

Published by Books by Rene'

ISBN: 979-8-9997823-1-1 (Paperback)

LCCN: 2025919141

Cover design by Rene' Stanley

First edition 2025

https://booksbyrene.com

Contents

Dedication   1

Epigraph   2

1. The Fortress of One   3

2. The Antidote and the Antagonist   12

3. The Choice   27

4. The Sunday Morning Ghost   40

5. An Essay as a Weapon   53

6. The Gospel of Nothing   74

7. The Uncomfortable Truth   90

8. The Quiet   103

9. The Seed of Hope   114

10. The Cup of Tea   127

11. The Empathy of the Sage   135

12. The Terror of the Void   144

Discussion Questions for "Running from Sunday"   168

About the author   172

For everyone who has wrestled with grief
and found the courage to keep wrestling.

Epigraph

"And Jacob was left alone. And a man wrestled with him until the breaking of the day."

— Genesis 32:24

This story was born from the understanding that grief changes us in ways we never expect, and that sometimes the very faith that once sustained us can feel like another loss to mourn. If you have walked through the valley of sudden loss, struggled with doubt in sacred spaces, or found yourself vulnerable to those who would exploit your pain, please know that your experience is seen and honored in these pages.

Brianna's journey is not intended as a prescription for healing or a definitive statement about faith—it is simply one woman's wrestle with the impossible questions that loss brings. Some readers may find comfort in her path toward community and hope; others may find validation in her struggle with doubt and anger. Both responses are welcome here.

If these themes feel too tender for where you are in your own journey, please be gentle with yourself. Healing happens on no one's schedule but our own, and sometimes the most courageous thing we can do is close the book and return to it when we're ready. For those who continue reading, I hope you find something true in Brianna's story—not answers, perhaps, but companionship in the questions that matter most.

Chapter One

The Fortress of One

The key to surviving college, Brianna decided as she dragged her last suitcase up three flights of Hawthorne Hall stairs, was to need absolutely nothing from anyone.

The dorm room door stood open, already claiming her with the sound of someone humming—actually humming—while unpacking. Brianna paused in the hallway, her duffel bag cutting into her shoulder where the strap had been digging for three flights of stairs, her thighs still burning from hauling everything she owned up the narrow stairwell that reeked of industrial cleaner and something sour she couldn't name. Her shoulders automatically hunched as if bracing for a blow that had already landed months ago. Through the doorway, she could see her roommate's side of the room exploding into life: fairy lights being strung with the focused determination of someone who believed in making spaces beautiful, their warm glow stabbing at her eyes like tiny accusatory stars. The brightness made her skull ache. Potted plants lined up on the windowsill like tiny green soldiers of optimism, their leaves catching the afternoon sun that felt too sharp, too insistent. The humming continued—some pop song she half-recognized—weaving through the sounds of hangers scraping against the closet rod, drawers sliding open and shut, the rustle of tissue paper being smoothed and folded with care. Even the air in the room felt different: lighter, infused with vanilla body spray and the green smell of growing things, so foreign to the stale heaviness that had settled into her own lungs months ago.

Of course.

"Oh my gosh, you must be Bree!"

The voice belonged to a girl with dark, curly hair escaping from a messy bun and paint-stained fingers. She was holding what appeared to be a handmade banner that read "Welcome Home!" in looping, cheerful letters.

"Brianna," she corrected, her voice flat and final. Not Bree. Never Bree again. That name belonged to her mother—whispered in bedtime stories, called out across playgrounds, spoken with such tenderness it used to make her chest warm. Bree was the daughter who'd believed in forever, who'd curled up in hospital chairs and held her mother's hand through chemo sessions, promising they'd beat this together. That girl had died in a room that smelled like antiseptic and broken promises, buried alongside the woman who'd given her that name. Brianna was armor—sharp consonants and formal distance, a name that couldn't be softened into pet names or wielded like a weapon of intimacy. Brianna was who she'd chosen to become: someone untouchable, someone who couldn't be destroyed by love again.

"I'm Maya! I was so excited when I got your roommate assignment. I looked you up on Facebook and saw you're from Crestwood—I have a cousin there! Small world, right?"

Brianna's stomach clenched. Crestwood meant church directories and family friends and people who would tilt their heads with that particular expression of pity and say things like "How are you *holding up*?" in voices soft with practiced sympathy.

"Right." She hefted her suitcase onto the bare mattress that would be hers for the next nine months. The institutional bedframe was identical to Maya's, but where her roommate's was already dressed in a colorful quilt that looked handmade, Brianna's remained starkly functional. She preferred it that way.

Maya seemed to take this as encouragement. "I brought some extra decorations if you want to borrow anything. I always go a little overboard, but I figure if you're going to live somewhere for a year, it should feel like—"

"I'm good." Brianna unzipped her suitcase with more force than necessary. Inside: gray comforter, black sheets, three band t-shirts she'd bought specifically because she'd never heard their music, and a poster for a movie about the meaninglessness of existence that she'd ordered online the day after the funeral. "I don't really do the whole... decorating thing."

She could feel Maya's eyes on her as she methodically began creating her side of the room. Where Maya had explosion, Brianna would have void. Where Maya had color, she would have gray. It felt like the most honest thing she'd done in months.

"That's cool too," Maya said, and something in her tone made Brianna glance over. The other girl was still smiling, but it was softer now, less manic cheerfulness and more something that looked almost like understanding. "Sometimes simple is better."

Brianna's phone buzzed against her leg. A text from her father: How's the move-in going, kiddo? Your mom would have been so proud to see you starting this new chapter.

The words hit like a physical blow, stealing the air from her lungs. Her mother would have been here three hours early, armed with color-coded storage bins and that lavender fabric softener that made everything smell like home. She would have cried the moment they pulled into the parking lot—happy tears, proud tears, terrified tears all tangled together. She would have insisted on making the bed herself, tucking the corners with military precision while rattling off a stream of reminders: call every Sunday, eat vegetables, don't walk alone at night, remember you are loved loved loved. She would have lingered in the doorway, memorizing everything, her hand pressed to her heart the way she did when emotions overwhelmed her small frame.

Brianna's chest constricted, her throat closing around a sound that wasn't quite a sob. The phantom scent of lavender made her dizzy. Maya was still chattering somewhere behind her, but the words dissolved into white noise as grief crashed over her in waves—sudden, merciless, complete.

She shoved the phone back into her pocket without responding, her fingers trembling as she forced her lungs to remember how to breathe.

"Everything okay?" Maya asked.

"Fine." Brianna pulled her new comforter from its packaging, the gray fabric unfolding like storm clouds. She'd specifically chosen the most depressing color possible. "Just my dad checking in."

"That's sweet. My parents called like six times on the drive here. I think my mom cried more than I did when they left."

The casual mention of a mother who was alive, who called, who cried at normal things like college drop-offs, hit Brianna like a physical blow. She focused on spreading the comforter with military precision, making sure every corner was perfectly aligned.

"Are they coming to the parent orientation thing tomorrow?" Maya continued, apparently oblivious to the way Brianna had gone completely still.

"No." The word came out sharper than she'd intended. "My dad had to work."

It wasn't technically a lie. Her father did have to work—he'd been throwing himself into sixty-hour weeks since the funeral, anything to avoid the silence of their house. But the truth was, she'd told him not to come. The idea of walking around campus with him, both of them pretending this was a normal milestone instead of an escape route, was unbearable.

"Oh, that sucks. Well, if you want to hang out during any of the orientation stuff, I'm totally up for it. I already signed us up for the roommate scavenger hunt thing—I hope that's okay?"

Brianna turned, a refusal already forming on her lips, but Maya was back to hanging fairy lights, humming again, and something about the casual assumption of companionship caught her off guard. When was the last time someone had just... included her in something? Assumed she might want to participate in normal college things?

Don't, she warned herself. *Don't get attached. Don't let her get attached.*

"I'm probably going to be pretty busy," she said instead. "You know, getting settled and stuff."

"Sure, no worries. The offer stands if you change your mind."

Maya plugged in the fairy lights, and suddenly her side of the room was bathed in warm, golden light that made everything look softer, more magical. It was exactly the kind of thing Brianna would have loved a year ago. The kind of thing she and her mother would have spent an hour arranging together, stepping back to admire their work, her mom making suggestions about where to hang pictures and whether they needed more plants.

Now it just looked like a mockery.

She turned back to her own side, pulling out the band poster and tacking it to the wall without ceremony. The black and white image of four angry-looking guys stared back at her with appropriate disdain for everything around them.

"I love their sound," Maya said, and Brianna tensed, waiting for the lie to be exposed. "Super raw and honest, you know?"

Brianna made a noncommittal noise. Raw and honest. That was one way to put it.

Her phone buzzed again. This time it was a text from Pastor Mike, her old youth pastor: *Praying for you today, Bree! College is such an exciting adventure. Can't wait to hear how God is going to use this time in your life.*

She deleted it without reading it twice.

"I'm going to go grab some coffee from downstairs," Maya announced, apparently finishing whatever project she'd been working on. "Want me to bring you some? I think they have those fancy flavored creamers."

"I'm good."

Maya paused, her fingers drumming once against her laptop before she closed it. "You sure? I'm buying."

There was something different in Maya's voice now—not her usual bright chatter, but something quieter. More careful. The kind of tone that came from knowing when to push and when to simply stand nearby, ready. It reminded Brianna uncomfortably of her mother's gentle persistence, the way she'd offer tea during late-night study sessions or suggest movies after bad days, always casual on the surface but somehow conveying that the door would stay open as long as needed.

"I said I'm good."

Maya nodded, gathering her things with deliberate slowness. "Okay. But I'm getting an extra cup anyway—you know how I am with caffeine decisions." She headed toward the door, then glanced back with a small smile that didn't quite reach her eyes. "It'll just be sitting there if you change your mind."

Maya nodded, grabbing her wallet and key. "Okay. I'll be back in a bit. Oh, and Bree?"

Brianna's jaw clenched. "Brianna."

"Sorry, Brianna. I just wanted to say—I know roommate situations can be weird, and I don't want you to feel like you have to be my best friend or anything. But if you need anything, even if it's just someone to vent to about professors or whatever, I'm here. No strings attached."

The words hit Brianna like a physical blow, unexpected in their gentleness. Something deep in her chest cracked—just a hairline fracture, but enough to let in a sliver of warmth she hadn't felt in months. Her throat tightened traitorously, and for one terrifying second, she almost said *thank you*. Almost let herself believe that someone could offer kindness without expecting her to shatter completely in return.

But then the familiar panic surged, cold and protective. *No strings attached*—that's what they all said, until the strings appeared anyway, until caring became obligation became disappointment became loss. The old Brianna, the one who used to curl up with friends during movie marathons and share midnight confessions, stirred hopefully in her chest. But the new Brianna—the one who knew better, who had learned the cost of letting people matter—slammed the door shut on that dangerous flutter of hope.

She pressed her lips together, rebuilding her walls brick by brick, even as something inside her screamed in protest.

Maya left before Brianna could formulate a response, the door clicking shut behind her with a soft finality.

Alone for the first time in hours, Brianna sank onto her perfectly made bed and looked around at what she'd created: a monument to nothing. Gray walls, gray bedding, angry music, and empty space where normal college students would put photos of friends and family and all the people they'd miss while they were away.

She pulled out her phone and scrolled to her father's text, her thumb hovering over the keyboard. She should respond. She should tell him the room was fine, that Maya seemed nice, that everything was going according to plan.

Instead, she found herself opening her photo gallery, scrolling back to the last picture she'd taken of her mother. It was from Easter, just two weeks before the diagnosis that changed everything. Her mom was laughing at something Brianna's dad had said, her face bright with the kind of joy that seemed impossible now, her hand resting on Brianna's shoulder with casual, unconscious love.

"Your mom would have been so proud."

The words felt like salt in a wound that refused to heal. Her mom would have been proud of the old Brianna—the one who painted her nails bright pink and left glittery nail polish bottles scattered across her vanity, who would have squealed over Maya's fairy lights and spent twenty minutes arranging them just right before taking a dozen photos. The girl who stayed up too late dissecting every text from crushes, who called home not because she had to but because she missed the sound of her mother's laugh, who collected friends like souvenirs and sent breathless updates about dining hall drama and the cute boy in her psych class.

That girl had died in a hospital waiting room six months ago.

This new version—the one who hadn't touched makeup since the funeral, who flinched away from laughter like it was something obscene, who chose the gray walls and empty spaces because color felt like a betrayal—this wasn't someone her mother would recognize. And the cruelest part was that somewhere, buried under all this numbness, Brianna knew her mom would have loved even this broken version. Would have sat on this bare mattress and held her while she shattered, would have understood that sometimes you have to become a stranger to yourself just to survive the weight of missing someone.

But she couldn't bear to believe in that kind of unconditional love. Not when accepting it meant accepting that her mother was really gone.

So she chose to be unrecognizable instead. If she became someone else entirely—someone cold and untouchable—then maybe the girl who had lost everything could disappear too.

Brianna closed the photo and shoved her phone into her desk drawer, burying it under a stack of notebooks. Then she pulled out her headphones, put them on, and turned the music up loud enough to drown out the sound of Maya's humming still echoing in her memory.

Outside her window, she could see other students moving around campus with their parents, taking pictures, laughing, crying happy tears at this milestone moment. Normal families doing normal things.

She closed the blinds and turned toward the wall, shutting it all out.

The fortress of one was complete.

Chapter Two

The Antidote and the Antagonist

The student involvement fair was exactly the kind of chaos Brianna had hoped to avoid.

She stood at the edge of the quad, her damp palm crushing a schedule she didn't want, the paper corners cutting into her fingers as she watched hundreds of students swarm between brightly colored booths like frenzied bees drunk on nectar. The September air hit her in waves—first the cloying sweetness of fresh-baked cookies from the Campus Ministry table that made her stomach lurch, then the acrid grease from food trucks that coated the back of her throat, all underlaid with the sharp tang of sweat and the metallic desperation that seemed to radiate from large groups of eighteen-year-olds shouting over each other to reinvent themselves. The cacophony pressed against her eardrums—laughter too loud, music bleeding from competing speakers, the scrape of folding chairs on concrete—until every sound felt like it was happening inside her skull, making her want to press her hands over her ears and run.

Maya had left an hour ago with a stack of flyers thick enough to choke a horse and enough enthusiasm to power the entire electrical grid. "Just walk around!" she'd chirped. "See what speaks to you!"

Nothing spoke to Brianna except the bench near the library where she could sit alone and fulfill her promise to her father that she'd "get involved." Technically, she was involved—she was here, wasn't she? She was observing. That counted.

"This is all performative bull, you know."

The voice drifted from behind her, low and lazily amused. She turned to find someone about her age lounging against a tree with practiced indifference, watching the fair like he was studying some mildly interesting social experiment. Dark hair fell across his forehead in a way that suggested he'd never owned a comb, and his faded Nirvana shirt bore the kind of authentic wear that couldn't be manufactured. Everything about him radiated the quiet confidence of someone who'd never felt the need to perform for anyone.

"Excuse me?"

He gestured toward the booths with a lazy wave. "All of it. The clubs, the activities, the 'finding your passion' propaganda. It's just another way to convince people they need to be constantly productive, constantly engaged, constantly performing their happiness for everyone else."

Something in Brianna's chest loosened. Finally—someone who saw through the bull.

"You're not wrong," she said, surprising herself by engaging.

He pushed off from the tree and moved closer, and she caught the scent of coffee and something else—cigarettes, maybe, or just the general aura of someone who didn't care about making good impressions.

"Liam," he said, extending a hand.

"Brianna."

His handshake was firm, brief, respectful of boundaries. She appreciated that.

"So what brings you to the festival of false promises?" he asked. "Parental pressure or genuine masochistic tendencies?"

Despite everything, Brianna felt her mouth twitch toward what might have been a smile. "Roommate guilt."

"Ah, the worst kind. Let me guess—she's already joined twelve clubs and wants you to 'put yourself out there.'"

"Fifteen clubs. And yes."

Liam laughed, a sound that was more cynical than joyful but somehow felt more honest than Maya's constant brightness. "I'm hiding from my orientation leader. Apparently, I'm supposed to be 'embracing the Northwood experience' right now instead of questioning whether any of this actually matters."

They stood in comfortable silence for a moment, watching a group of sorority girls try to convince a nervous-looking freshman that Greek life would "change her life forever."

"It's all so..." Brianna searched for the word.

"Desperate?" Liam supplied. "Like everyone's trying so hard to convince themselves that collecting activities will somehow fill whatever hole they're carrying around."

The words hit closer to home than she expected. She glanced at him sharply, but his expression remained casually philosophical, not probing.

"You sound like you speak from experience," she said.

"Don't we all? I mean, why else would we be here? Nobody shows up to college completely whole and functional. We're all running from something or toward something, usually both at the same time."

There was something unsettling about how clearly he saw through everything—including, potentially, her. But instead of feeling exposed, she felt understood. Here was someone who wouldn't expect her to perform gratitude or enthusiasm or any of the other emotions everyone else seemed to think she owed the world.

"So what are you running from?" she asked.

His smile turned sharper. "The myth of inherent meaning. The delusion that any of this—" he gestured broadly at the campus around them "—actually matters in any cosmic sense. You?"

The question hung in the air between them. She could deflect, change the subject, walk away. But something about his casual nihilism felt like permission to be equally honest.

"God," she said simply.

Liam's eyebrows rose, but not in judgment. More like recognition. "Ah. The ultimate authority figure. What did he do to earn your ire?"

The casual way he said it—not "how could you say that" or "have you tried praying about it" but simple acknowledgment that God might, indeed, be worthy of anger—made something tight in her chest uncoil.

"Took my mom," she said, the words coming out flat and matter-of-fact. "Six months ago. After I spent two years begging him to save her."

"And let me guess—everyone told you it was part of his plan?"

The bitter laugh that escaped her surprised them both. "Among other platitudes, yes."

"Jesus. I mean, not literally Jesus, obviously, since we've established he's persona non grata. But that's some premium-grade bull right there."

It was exactly what she needed to hear. Not sympathy, not attempts to reframe her loss as somehow meaningful, just acknowledgment that yes, it was bull. Pure, unadulterated bull.

"Tell me about it."

"You know what the real kicker is?" Liam continued, warming to his theme. "They act like questioning the whole system makes you broken instead of, you know, intellectually honest. Like blind faith is somehow more virtuous than demanding actual evidence for extraordinary claims."

Brianna found herself nodding. "Right? I spent eighteen years being told that doubt was the enemy, that if I just believed hard enough, everything would work out. And then it didn't, and suddenly it was my fault for not having enough faith."

"Classic victim-blaming. It's the same mechanism they use in all authoritarian systems—convince people that their suffering is somehow their own fault so they won't question the people in power."

The words felt like cool water on a burn she hadn't realized was still raw. Here was someone who could take her anger and give it an intellectual framework, who could transform her pain from personal failure into philosophical clarity.

"I should probably warn you," she said, "I'm pretty toxic company these days. Most people find my worldview a little too dark."

Liam's smile was slow and appreciative. "Toxic is just what boring people call honesty. Besides, darkness is underrated. It's where you can actually see the stars."

The metaphor was pretty, almost romantic, and for a moment Brianna felt something flutter in her chest that wasn't anger or grief. Something that felt almost like attraction, or at least the memory of what attraction used to feel like.

"So what's your major?" she asked, suddenly wanting to keep the conversation going.

"Philosophy with a focus on existentialism. Because apparently, I enjoy torturing myself with questions that have no answers. You?"

"Undecided. I was going to do social work, but..." She trailed off, not wanting to explain that helping people had been tied up in her faith, and her faith had been tied up in her mother, and her mother was gone.

"But then you realized that most social problems are just symptoms of larger systemic issues that can't be solved by individual intervention?"

It wasn't exactly what she'd been thinking, but it was close enough. "Something like that."

"Makes sense. Why put a band-aid on a severed artery, right?"

They were interrupted by a girl with a clipboard and an aggressively cheerful smile. "Hi there! Are you guys interested in learning about Campus Crusade for Christ? We have free pizza!"

The girl's eyes landed on the small cross necklace Brianna still wore out of habit rather than faith, and her smile brightened. "Oh, I love your necklace! Are you a believer?"

Brianna's hand flew to her throat, fingers closing around the silver chain with a grip that was almost violent. The cross seemed to pulse against her palm, suddenly heavy as a stone, burning through her skin like a brand. She'd forgotten she was still wearing it—eighteen years of muscle memory, her mother's voice echoing from some distant Sunday morning: *Never leave the house without it, sweetheart. It'll keep you safe.*

Safe. The word twisted in her chest like a knife.

Her mother had pressed it into her palm the night before her confirmation, the delicate silver warm from being clutched in trembling hands. "This was your grandmother's," she'd whispered, fastening the chain around Brianna's neck with reverent fingers. "And now it's yours. Promise me you'll never take it off." The tiny diamonds had caught the lamplight, winking like stars, like promises, like lies.

Now the cross felt like it was choking her, the chain a noose of memory and guilt. She wanted to rip it off, to hurl it across the room and watch it shatter against the wall—but her fingers wouldn't obey. They trembled against the silver, caught between fury and desperation, between the girl who had knelt at that altar with such blazing faith and the woman who now stood hollow, abandoned by the very God her mother had sworn would never leave her side.

The necklace was all she had left. The last thread connecting her to a woman six feet underground and a faith that had crumbled to ash in her hands.

"I—" she started, but Liam smoothly stepped in.

"We're actually exploring some of the more intellectually rigorous options," he said with a polite smile that didn't reach his eyes. "You know, clubs that encourage questions rather than providing pre-packaged answers."

The girl's smile faltered slightly. "Well, we encourage questions too! Faith is about seeking and—"

"Thanks, but we're good," Brianna said, her voice sharper than she'd intended. Her fingers were still wrapped around the cross, and she could feel its edges pressing into her palm.

The girl looked between them uncertainly, then moved on to easier targets.

"Smooth," Liam said approvingly. "Though I'm surprised you didn't just tell her where she could stick her salvation."

Brianna's laugh came out bitter. "Old habits. Six months ago, I would have been the one with the clipboard."

"Really? You were one of them?"

The way he said it should have been offensive, but somehow it felt validating instead. Like he was acknowledging the magnitude of her transformation.

"Youth group leader, mission trip veteran, the whole nine yards. I was going to change the world through the power of love and Jesus."

"What changed?"

She looked at him—really looked at him. His dark eyes were focused entirely on her, not with the careful sympathy she'd grown to hate, but with genuine curiosity. Like her story was interesting rather than tragic.

"Reality," she said simply.

"The great destroyer of beautiful illusions."

"Something like that."

Her phone buzzed in her pocket, and she glanced at it reflexively. A text from Maya: Found the perfect club for you! Environmental Justice Coalition meets Thursdays. Very your vibe!

The assumption that Maya knew anything about her "vibe" was irritating, but what bothered her more was the little flutter of warmth that came with knowing her roommate was thinking about her.

"Let me guess," Liam said, reading her expression. "Someone who still believes in the power of positive thinking?"

"My roommate. She's..." Brianna searched for words that wouldn't sound cruel. "Optimistic."

"Ah. One of those people who thinks the universe is fundamentally good and everything happens for a reason?"

"Pretty much."

"Those are the most dangerous ones. They mean well, but they can't accept that some things are just meaningless and terrible. They'll try to find silver linings in your trauma until you want to scream." His voice carried that edge of certainty I'd been craving—someone who finally got it. But something about the way he said "dangerous," so quick and final, made me glance back at Maya's retreating figure. She was laughing at something her friend said, completely oblivious to being dissected. The word felt too big, too sharp for someone whose worst crime was offering cookies and hope.

The accuracy of this assessment was startling. Maya hadn't done anything wrong, exactly, but there was something about her relentless cheer that felt like pressure—like an expectation that Brianna should be healing faster, trying harder, finding ways to be grateful for this "new chapter" everyone kept insisting college would be.

"She left me coffee this morning," Brianna said. "Without asking. Just left it on my desk with a little note about having a great day."

"And that pissed you off?"

"It should have been nice. It was nice. But it felt like..." She struggled to articulate the feeling. "Like she was trying to fix me with caffeine and kindness."

"The tyranny of other people's care," Liam said, nodding sagely. "They can't stand to see you in pain, not because they actually want to help you process it, but because your pain makes them uncomfortable. So they try to paper over it with small gestures that make them feel better about themselves."

This was exactly what she'd been unable to put into words. The way Maya's kindness felt like a demand for gratitude, a subtle pressure to be the kind of person who could be cheered up by fairy lights and herbal tea.

"You get it," she said, and meant it.

"I get a lot of things. Comes with the territory of not believing in comforting lies."

A comfortable silence fell between them as they watched the chaos of the fair continue around them. Students rushed from booth to booth, collecting information about clubs they'd probably never join, trying to construct identities from extracurricular activities.

"So what now?" Brianna asked. "Do we just stand here judging everyone, or do you have somewhere else you need to be?"

"I was thinking of grabbing coffee and continuing this conversation somewhere with fewer people trying to save our souls. You interested?"

The invitation hung in the air between them. She could say no, go back to her room, continue building her fortress of solitude. It would be safer that way.

But something about Liam felt like an antidote to everything she'd been struggling with—the well-meaning sympathy, the pressure to heal, the expectation that she should find meaning in her suffering. He offered something different: permission to be angry, validation for her cynicism, intellectual companionship without emotional demands.

"Yeah," she said. "I'm interested."

Walking away from the fair, Brianna felt something shift inside her chest—a loosening she hadn't experienced in months. Not happiness, exactly. Relief. Like finally hearing someone speak her native language after years of stilted translation.

The Campus Ministry booth faded behind them, volunteers still hawking free pizza and salvation to anyone who'd listen. Brianna had choked down enough salvation to last several lifetimes.

But this—honest, unvarnished truth, intellectually rigorous despair—this was what her mind had been starving for. What felt, for the first time in forever, like nourishment.

***

Twenty minutes later, they were settled in a corner booth at the coffee shop just off campus, tucked away from the fluorescent glare and forced cheer of the student center. The place felt like a deliberate rejection of the world outside—exposed brick walls scarred with decades of paint and posters, furniture that looked salvaged from estate sales and breakups, each piece carrying the weight of other people's abandoned lives. Brianna sank into the cracked vinyl of the booth, its worn surface molding to her body like an old confession, and wrapped her hands around her black coffee. No cream to cloud it, no sugar to sweeten the harsh truth of it—just bitter darkness that matched the hollow ache in her chest. Around them, conversations blurred into white noise, punctuated by the hiss of the espresso machine and the scrape of chairs against uneven floors. Afternoon light filtered through grimy windows, casting everything in amber shadows that made the world feel muted, softer at the edges. Here, listening to Liam deconstruct the philosophical underpinnings of organized religion in that voice like velvet over steel, she could almost forget the brightness waiting outside—all those smiling faces and easy answers that felt like lies against her skin.

"The whole concept of faith is..." Liam paused, swirling his espresso thoughtfully. "I don't know, it just feels like intellectual surrender to me. Dressed up as virtue." He looked up at her, his expression more questioning than certain. "I mean, think about it—they're asking you to believe things without evidence, and somehow that's supposed to be more noble than actually wanting proof?"

"But what about the community aspect?" Brianna found herself asking, then immediately wondered why she was playing devil's advocate. "I mean, some people seem to find real comfort in it."

Liam's smile was patient, like a teacher explaining something to a slow student. "Comfort isn't truth. You can find community anywhere—you don't need to believe in magic to belong somewhere. All religion does is create artificial barriers between insiders and outsiders, then convince people they need those barriers to feel safe."

The words resonated, but something about them also made her uncomfortable in a way she couldn't name. Maybe it was the dismissive way he said "magic," or the certainty in his voice, or the fact that he'd never actually lost the thing he was so confidently deconstructing.

"But then he leaned forward, his dark eyes intense, and said, "The real question is: what do you do with the anger? Because that's the part they never tell you—that losing faith doesn't make the pain go away, it just takes away the framework you used to make sense of it."

And just like that, he was speaking directly to the core of her struggle. But something about the way he'd moved closer made her pulse quicken—not entirely from recognition. There was a hunger in his gaze that felt both magnetic and predatory, like he was feeding off her pain rather than simply understanding it. His words were exactly what she needed to hear, which should have been comforting. Instead, a small voice whispered that maybe he knew her struggle so intimately because he was drowning in the same dark waters, and she couldn't decide if that made him her lifeline or the undertow that would pull her deeper."

The anger was the hardest part, the thing that felt too big for her body, too hot for her skin. Everyone wanted her to move through it, past it, beyond it. But Liam was the first person to suggest that maybe the anger itself was valuable.

"I don't know," she admitted. "I feel like I'm going to explode most of the time."

"Good. Anger is clarity. It's your mind rejecting bull narratives and demanding something real. Don't let anyone convince you to let go of it before you're ready."

The permission to stay angry felt like the first honest thing anyone had offered her in months.

"So what's your story?" she asked. "What made you so... clear about all this?"

Liam's expression darkened slightly. "Grew up in a family where Sunday morning was mandatory and questions were discouraged. Spent my teenage years watching my parents use their faith as an excuse for some pretty spectacular hypocrisy. By the time I got to college, I was ready to think for myself."

It wasn't the same as losing someone, but Brianna could hear the pain underneath his casual tone. Maybe that was what drew her to him—the sense that he'd also been betrayed by something he'd once trusted.

Her phone buzzed again. This time it was her father: Hope you're having a good first day, sweetheart. Love you.

The endearment made her chest tight. He'd been trying so hard since the funeral, reaching out more than he ever had when her mother was alive to facilitate their communication. It felt like too little, too late, and also like more pressure than she could handle.

"Family?" Liam asked, noticing her expression.

"My dad. He's been... hovering since my mom died. I think he feels guilty that they left me to deal with all the hospital stuff while he worked."

"Guilt is a useless emotion," Liam said matter-of-factly. "It doesn't change anything, and it just makes people act weird around you. My parents went through a phase of trying to make up for years of emotional neglect after I told them I didn't believe anymore. Suddenly they wanted to have deep conversations and understand my perspective. Too little, too late, you know?"

Brianna nodded, though something about the comparison felt off. Her father's texts weren't manipulative or guilt-driven—they were just... sad. Like he was trying to figure out how to be a parent to the daughter who remained.

But Liam was already moving on, launching into a story about his philosophy professor who'd assigned Nietzsche to a classroom full of former

Catholic school students, and Brianna let herself be carried along by his voice, his certainty, his refusal to find silver linings in anything.

For the first time since arriving at college, she felt like she could breathe.

Outside the coffee shop window, other students walked by in groups, laughing and talking about normal college things. But inside their corner booth, Brianna and Liam constructed a different kind of space—one where darkness was acceptable, where anger was intelligent, where the absence of God felt like freedom instead of abandonment.

It felt dangerous and exhilarating and exactly like what she needed.

When they finally parted ways two hours later, Liam's hand brushed hers as he helped her with her jacket.

"Same time tomorrow?" he asked. "I'm thinking we tackle the myth of inherent human goodness."

"It's a date," Brianna said, then immediately wondered if she'd meant it literally.

From the way Liam smiled—slow and knowing and just a little predatory—she suspected he hoped she had.

Walking back to her dorm as the sun set over campus, Brianna felt something she hadn't experienced in months: anticipation. Not for healing or moving forward or any of the other things people kept insisting she should want, but for the simple pleasure of spending time with someone who understood that some things were irredeemably broken, and that was okay.

"Her phone buzzed one more time as she climbed the stairs to her room. Maya: How was the fair? No pressure to answer if you're not ready to talk about it yet.

Brianna paused in the stairwell, her thumb hovering over the keyboard. She could mention Liam, try to explain what it felt like to find someone who didn't want to fix her. The careful space Maya had left in her message caught her off guard—when had Maya learned to read between the lines like that? But even knowing Maya might understand more than she'd given her credit for, Brianna still couldn't find the words. Maya, with her fairy lights and her coffee offerings and her relentless faith that everything would work out fine—maybe she saw more than Brianna had realized, but that didn't make the gap between them any easier to cross."

Instead, she typed back: Yeah. I think I did.

It wasn't a lie, exactly. She had found something interesting.

Something that might save her. Or tear her apart completely.

But for the first time in months, Brianna found herself genuinely curious about the answer.

Chapter Three

The Choice

"Friday night slammed into Brianna like a verdict she wasn't ready to hear."

She sat cross-legged on her narrow dorm bed, her stomach knotted as she stared at two text messages that felt like competing manifestos for her soul. Maya's invitation glowed softly from her phone screen, each word carefully chosen: "Hey! The Well is having a super casual hangout tonight - just pizza, games, and getting to know people. Want to come? No pressure at all, but I thought it might be fun! " Even through the screen, Brianna could feel Maya's gentle intuition at work - the way she'd sensed Brianna's hesitation at orientation, how she'd positioned this not as an obligation but as a gift she could unwrap or leave unopened. It was an invitation into belonging without demanding she prove herself worthy first.

Below it, Liam's message pulsed with different energy entirely, sharp-edged and uncompromising: "Party at Delta Chi tonight. Real one, not some sanitized orientation bull. You in?" His words carried the weight of judgment, dividing her world into the authentic and the performative, daring her to choose which side she belonged on. In his universe, Maya's careful kindness would be weakness, her thoughtful approach just another layer of institutional fakeness.

Brianna's hands trembled slightly as she held the phone. Her throat felt tight, her chest constricted, as if the weight of who she might become was physically pressing down on her ribs. One message promised safety in community; the other, truth through rebellion. Both felt like doors that, once opened, might never close again.

The contrast was so stark it was almost funny. Maya's careful emoji and gentle disclaimer versus Liam's assumption that she'd want to dive headfirst into whatever chaos he was offering. Six months ago, the choice would have been obvious—she'd have been the girl suggesting the pizza hangout, probably bringing homemade cookies and a guitar for impromptu worship songs.

Now, the thought of sitting in a circle with bright-eyed freshmen sharing their testimonies made her skin crawl.

"Maya was at her desk across the room, highlighter in hand as she color-coded her planner with the kind of meticulous care that suggested organization was a form of prayer. Her fairy lights cast warm shadows across textbooks and sticky notes covered in cheerful reminders: "Call Mom Sunday!" and "Coffee with Sarah from Bio!" But tucked beneath the brightness were quieter details—a dog-eared copy of *Man's Search for Meaning* bookmarked three-quarters through, a handwritten note that read "Dad's chemo - Tues 2pm" in smaller, more careful script. The sight should have been comforting. Instead, it felt like looking at a museum exhibit: Normal College Girl Who Has Learned That Sometimes You Have to Build Your Own Light, circa before everything went to hell. Every colorful sticky note, every perfectly planned coffee date—it wasn't naivety. It was architecture. Maya had constructed this brightness the way others built walls, one deliberate act of kindness at a time."

"So," Maya said without looking up from her rainbow-coded schedule, "got any plans tonight?"

The question was casual, but Brianna caught the slight tension in her roommate's shoulders, the way she gripped her highlighter just a little too tightly. Maya had been trying so hard to give her space while still leaving doors open, and something about that careful balance made Brianna's chest tighten with guilt she didn't want to feel.

"Actually, yeah." Brianna's thumb hovered over Liam's message. "There's this party."

Maya's highlighter paused mid-stroke. She glanced up with a small smile. "Fun. Where at?"

"Some guy's place. Liam." Brianna shifted, suddenly aware of how little she actually knew. "I just met him yesterday."

"Ah." Maya's tone stayed light, but she set down her highlighter entirely now. "What's he like?"

"I don't know. Different, I guess."

"Good different or..." Maya let the question hang, eyebrows raised just enough to show she was asking as a friend, not interrogating.

Brianna struggled to find words that wouldn't sound like a rejection of everything Maya represented. "He doesn't try to fix things. Or find meaning in everything. He just lets things be what they are."

Maya set down her highlighter and turned in her chair, giving Brianna her full attention. "That sounds... refreshing, actually."

The response caught Brianna off guard. She'd expected Maya to launch into some speech about the importance of hope or the danger of cynical influences. Instead, her roommate's expression was thoughtful, almost wistful.

"Yeah," Brianna said carefully. "It is."

"Well, be safe, okay? And text me if you need anything. I'll probably just be hanging out at The Well anyway—nothing exciting."

The casual mention of The Well sent a familiar spike of irritation through Brianna's chest, followed immediately by something that felt uncomfortably like longing. She could picture it: students sitting in a circle on mismatched couches, sharing pizza and talking about their weeks, someone inevitably pulling out a guitar for the kind of acoustic worship songs that used to make her feel like she was floating. The image was so vivid it made her throat tight.

"What's it like?" she found herself asking. "The Well, I mean."

Maya's face lit up, then immediately dimmed as if she was trying to contain her enthusiasm. "It's... I don't know, it's not what you'd expect, maybe? It's not like youth group or anything formal. People just hang out, talk about whatever's on their minds. Sometimes we pray together, but it's not required or anything. Mostly it just feels like having family dinner with people who actually want to be there."

Family dinner. The words hit like a physical blow, conjuring memories of Sunday meals that stretched for hours, her mother insisting they go around the table sharing the best part of their week while her father rolled his eyes but participated anyway. The way her mom would reach across the table to squeeze her hand during the prayer, the comfortable chaos of passing dishes and interrupting each other and belonging somewhere so completely it felt like breathing.

Maya must have seen something change in her expression because she quickly added, "But parties can be fun too! I hope you have a good time."

Brianna nodded, not trusting her voice. Her phone buzzed again—Liam, probably wondering where she was. The party would be loud enough to drown out memories, chaotic enough to keep her from thinking about family dinners or worship songs or any of the other things that felt like betrayals of her grief.

"I should get ready," she said, standing abruptly.

"Of course! Oh, and Bree—I mean, Brianna—" Maya caught herself, wincing slightly. "Just... you know where to find me if you change your mind about anything."

The offer hung in the air between them, weighted with more than just tonight's plans. Brianna could feel Maya watching as she pulled clothes from her dresser—the black jeans that made her feel armored, the band t-shirt that announced her allegiance to nothing, the jacket that smelled faintly of the perfume her mother used to wear because she couldn't bring herself to wash it.

As she changed, she caught sight of herself in the small mirror above her dresser. The girl looking back was all sharp angles and defensive posture, her dark hair hanging like a curtain she could hide behind. She looked like someone who belonged at the kind of party Liam was promising—someone who'd traded her youth group t-shirts for something harder, more honest.

Someone her mother wouldn't recognize.

The thought should have hurt, but instead it felt like victory.

"See you later," she said to Maya, who was already back to her color-coding, though Brianna noticed she kept glancing toward the door.

The walk across campus felt like crossing a border between two countries. Behind her, the dorms glowed with the warm light of students settling in for quiet Friday nights—study groups and movie marathons and the kind of wholesome fun that felt like a foreign language now. Ahead, music pulsed from the off-campus houses where different rules applied, where the air itself seemed thicker with possibility and danger.

Liam was waiting for her at the corner of Greek Row, leaning against a streetlight with the casual confidence of someone who'd never doubted his place in the world—or had practiced this exact pose in his dorm room mirror. He'd changed from his afternoon philosophy-student uniform into dark jeans and a shirt that clung just enough to suggest he knew exactly how he looked, though she caught him adjusting the collar as she approached.

"I was starting to think you'd chickened out," he said, pushing off from the light to meet her. The movement was smooth, but his eyes searched her face for a reaction, as if her opinion mattered more than his tone suggested.

"Just fashionably late."

"Good. Punctuality is the virtue of the boring." The line came out too rehearsed, like something he'd read in a book about being interesting. He fell into step beside her, close enough that she could smell his cologne—something expensive and slightly dangerous that made her pulse quicken, though she wondered if he'd researched "colognes that suggest intellectual rebellion" online. "You look perfect, by the way. Like you're ready to burn something down."

There was something in the way he said it that made her skin prickle—not entirely unpleasantly, but with the recognition that he'd already written her character in his head. The girl who'd torch convention. The manic pixie to his brooding philosopher. His smile held a hint of satisfaction, as if her appearance had confirmed some theory he'd been testing.

The compliment sent warmth flooding through her chest, followed immediately by a flicker of unease. When was the last time someone had looked at her like that? Like she was something worth wanting instead of something that needed fixing?

"So what should I expect?" she asked as they approached a house that seemed to vibrate with bass lines and laughter.

"Chaos. Loud music. Cheap beer. College students pretending they know who they are." Liam's smile was sharp in the streetlight. "And hopefully some conversations that don't involve anyone asking what your major is or where you're from."

The front door was propped open, spilling light and sound onto the front porch where clusters of students stood smoking cigarettes and having the kind of intense conversations that only happened after midnight or several drinks. Brianna felt eyes on her as they walked up the steps—not hostile, just curious, evaluating. She straightened her shoulders and tried to look like she belonged in this world of deliberate carelessness and calculated rebellion.

Inside, the house was exactly what Liam had promised: controlled chaos. The living room furniture had been shoved against the walls like abandoned stage props, creating a makeshift dance floor where bodies moved without pretense—grinding, laughing, stumbling into each other with the kind of careless intimacy that only happened when no one was watching for social media. The strobing light from someone's cracked phone flashlight painted everything in harsh whites and deep shadows, making faces appear and disappear like fragments of a fever dream.

The air was a cocktail of contradictions: sweat and spilled beer, the sweet-sour tang of weed, someone's vanilla body spray mixing with the mustiness of old carpet. Music pounded from a bluetooth speaker duct-taped to a windowsill—not the carefully curated playlists Maya would have chosen, but raw, unfiltered sound that made conversation impossible unless you pressed your mouth directly to someone's ear and shouted your secrets into the dark.

"—don't give a crap what anyone thinks anymore—" a girl with purple hair screamed to her friend near the kitchen doorway, her words carrying the kind of brutal honesty that would never survive in Maya's world of calculated authenticity.

Someone stumbled into Brianna, beer sloshing from a red cup onto her shoes, and instead of the polite apology she expected, the stranger just grinned and kept dancing. No performance, no Instagram story, no careful documentation of the moment—just pure, messy existence.

It was the opposite of everything Brianna had been six months ago, and that felt like exactly the point. The chaos called to something hungry inside her, something that had been starving on a diet of perfect poses and filtered realities. But underneath the intoxicating freedom, a small voice whispered warnings about the morning after, when the music stopped and the real world demanded its pound of curated flesh.

Liam appeared at her elbow with two red solo cups, shouting something she couldn't hear over the music. She took the cup and drank without asking what was in it—some mixture of alcohol and fruit juice that burned going down but left a pleasant warmth in her stomach. Around them, students danced and laughed and lost themselves in the kind of temporary oblivion that felt like the most honest thing she'd encountered in months.

"Better than pizza and praise songs?" Liam asked, his mouth close to her ear so she could hear him.

Brianna took another drink, letting the alcohol blur the edges of her thoughts. Maya would be sitting in a circle right now, probably sharing something vulnerable and real while someone played guitar softly in the background. The image should have felt foreign, but instead it tugged at something deep in her chest—a longing for the kind of community she'd convinced herself she no longer wanted.

But here, pressed against Liam in the middle of a crowd of strangers, she didn't have to want anything. She could just be a body moving to music, a mouth drinking cheap alcohol, a girl who'd successfully burned down her old life and was dancing in the ashes.

"Much better," she said, and meant it.

Or at least, she meant to mean it.

The night fractured into fragments of sensation. Liam's palm pressed against the small of her back, steering her through bodies that swayed like wheat. Alcohol bloomed bitter on her tongue, chased by something sweeter—the metallic taste of freedom, sharp and unfamiliar.

Strangers leaned close with wine-stained smiles, their words washing over her in waves she didn't need to understand. They saw only her flushed cheeks and bright laugh, not the hollow spaces grief had carved beneath. Each new voice was a reprieve, each conversation a small amnesty from her own thoughts.

Drinks materialized in her hand—amber, clear, crimson—appearing whenever her fingers found empty air. She stopped asking their names, stopped counting their burn down her throat. The world tilted softer with each sip, edges blurring like watercolors in rain, until even her own pulse felt distant and dreamlike.

At some point, she found herself on the back porch, the cool night air a relief after the suffocating heat inside. Liam was beside her, closer than he'd been all evening, his shoulder pressed against hers as they watched other students stumble around the backyard.

"So," he said, his voice slightly slurred, "verdict on your first real college party?"

"It's..." Brianna searched for words through the pleasant fog in her head. "It's exactly what I needed."

"And what did you need?"

The question was weighted with more than casual curiosity. She could feel him watching her, waiting for something, and part of her brain—the part that wasn't swimming in alcohol—recognized that this was important somehow. That her answer mattered.

"To forget," she said simply. "To be someone else for a while."

"And who are you when you're someone else?"

She turned to look at him, really look at him, and saw something in his eyes that made her pulse quicken. Want. Interest. The kind of attention she'd forgotten she was capable of inspiring.

"I don't know yet," she said. "But I like her better than who I was before."

Liam's smile was slow, appreciative. "I like her too."

When he kissed her, it tasted like cheap beer and rebellion and the sharp thrill of becoming someone new—but underneath, something metallic and forced, like biting your tongue to prove you could stand the pain. His lips were chapped, moving with a practiced confidence that made her wonder how many other girls had stood in this exact spot, breathing in the same mix of cigarettes and cologne that clung to his leather jacket. For a moment, pressed against him in the darkness, Brianna felt like she was exactly where she belonged—not the girl who'd spent two years praying desperately for miracles that never came, but someone harder, more honest, more real. Yet even as she kissed him back with deliberate hunger, part of her felt like she was watching herself from above, performing rebellion rather than living it.

Her phone buzzed against her hip, probably Maya checking in like she had every night since the funeral, and Brianna's stomach clenched with something that might have been guilt. She could almost hear Maya's voice: *Just want to make sure you're okay. Call me back when you get this.* The same gentle persistence that had held Brianna together when everything else fell apart. But tonight was about forgetting, about choosing the noise and chaos and temporary oblivion over the quiet spaces where grief lived—even if it meant ignoring the one person who'd never stopped showing up. She pressed closer to him, letting the kiss deepen, drowning out the buzz of her phone and the whisper in her mind that sounded suspiciously like her old self, asking what she was really running from.

Tonight, she was exactly who she wanted to be.

Later, much later, when Liam walked her back to her dorm and kissed her goodnight with promises to call tomorrow, Brianna climbed the stairs to her room feeling like she was floating. The alcohol had worn off enough that she could walk straight, but the euphoria remained—the sense that she'd finally found something that fit.

She opened her door as quietly as possible, hoping Maya would be asleep. Instead, she found her roommate curled up in bed with a book, fairy lights casting gentle shadows across her face.

"Hey," Maya said softly, marking her place and setting the book aside. "How was the party?"

"Good," Brianna said, then immediately felt like the word was inadequate. "Really good, actually."

Maya smiled, and something about it looked almost relieved. "I'm glad. You deserve to have fun."

The simple statement hit Brianna unexpectedly hard. When was the last time someone had told her she deserved anything good? Most people seemed to think grief was supposed to be a full-time job, that finding moments of happiness somehow diminished the love she'd had for her mother.

"How was your thing?" she asked, settling on her bed and trying not to sway.

"Nice. Quiet. We talked about transition and change and how hard it is to figure out who you're supposed to be when everything familiar gets stripped away." Maya's voice was carefully neutral, but her eyes lingered on Brianna's face as she spoke. "About how some people try to control the pain by... controlling everything else. Making themselves smaller. Or disappearing entirely."

"Sounds heavy."

"Sometimes heavy is good." Maya chose her next words slowly, like she was placing stones across a river. "Sometimes it's exactly what you need to hear—that there are different ways to survive losing pieces of yourself. Healthy ways. Ways that don't require you to vanish."

They looked at each other across the small room, and for a moment Brianna felt the strange sense that they were having two conversations at once—the surface one about their respective evenings, and something deeper that made her chest tighten with recognition. Maya wasn't just describing some random group discussion. She was offering something, carefully wrapped in the safety of other people's stories. And Brianna could feel herself standing at the edge of understanding, knowing that if she stepped forward, she'd have to acknowledge what she'd been doing to herself. What she was still choosing to do. The weight of almost-recognition pressed against her ribs like a held breath, and she found herself looking away first.

"I'm glad you had a good time," Maya said again, reaching to turn off her bedside lamp. "Sleep well."

As her roommate settled into sleep, Brianna lay in her narrow bed staring at the ceiling, her head spinning slightly from alcohol and possibility. Tonight felt like a victory—proof that she could build a new life from the ashes of her old one, that she could find people who understood her anger instead of trying to heal it.

But as sleep began to pull her under, she found herself thinking about Maya's words: "Sometimes heavy is exactly what you need." And despite the success of the evening, despite Liam's kiss and the promise of more nights like this one, something deep in her chest ached with a longing she couldn't quite name.

She pushed the feeling away, focusing instead on the memory of Liam's hands, the taste of rebellion, the sound of her old self finally going quiet. These were victories, she told herself. Evidence of transformation.

Tomorrow, she would text him back. Tomorrow, she would continue becoming whoever this new version of herself was supposed to be. The words felt rehearsed, like lines from a script she'd memorized but never quite believed.

Tonight, she had chosen her path.

The fact that it felt less like choosing and more like falling—that the silence where her old self used to be echoed with something that might have been grief—was a problem for a different version of herself entirely. One who still cared about the difference between wanting something and needing to want it.

Chapter Four

The Sunday Morning Ghost

Saturday morning arrived like a hangover distilled into pure light and crystallized regret.

Brianna surfaced to Maya's careful movements—the whisper of turning pages, the porcelain kiss of mug against wood. Autumn sunlight pressed warm against her closed lids, nothing like last night's fluorescent brutality. This light remembered mercy. It carried the weight of Sunday mornings when her mother's voice would slip through a cracked door: "Church in an hour, sleepyhead."

But memory was already stirring, sharp-clawed and patient.

The memory hit before she could build her defenses against it, sharp and complete, like a fist to her solar plexus: her mother's silhouette in the doorway, already dressed in her favorite blue dress—the one with tiny white daisies that she'd bought on clearance and worn thin from too many Sunday mornings—her hair curled and pinned with the silver barrette Brianna had given her for Mother's Day three years ago, the one with the small chip on the left side that Mom had refused to replace because "it came from you, honey." The smell of coffee and cinnamon rolls drifting up from the kitchen, thick and warm, mixing with her mother's White

Shoulders perfume that still clung to everything she'd touched. Her father's voice calling from downstairs about finding his good shoes, the ones Mom had polished the night before and set by the door, and Mom's answering laugh—that quick, musical sound that always meant she was happy, truly happy—followed by the soft pad of her stockinged feet across the hardwood floor. The comfortable chaos of a family getting ready to worship together, the rustle of Sunday dress fabric, the clink of car keys, the way her mother always smoothed Brianna's hair one last time before they walked out the door, her palm warm and certain against her scalp.

"Morning service starts at ten-thirty, but I want to get there early to help set up communion," her mother would say, settling on the edge of Brianna's bed with that particular mix of patience and gentle insistence that meant resistance was futile. "And don't forget—Mrs. Patterson asked if you'd help with the children's choir today."

Brianna's chest constricted, her throat closing around a sound that wasn't quite a sob. She pressed her face deeper into her pillow, trying to suffocate the memory before it could fully bloom, but it was too late. The phantom scent of her mother's lavender perfume filled her nostrils, so vivid she actually turned her head to look for the source.

Nothing. Just Maya's careful movements and the accusatory brightness of Saturday morning pretending to be something it wasn't.

"You okay?" Maya's voice was soft, concerned. "You made a noise."

Brianna forced her eyes open, squinting against the light that felt too sharp, too insistent. Maya was sitting at her desk in pajamas and an oversized sweatshirt, surrounded by textbooks and what appeared to be a half-eaten bagel. Her hair was pulled back in a messy bun, and she had the slightly rumpled look of someone who'd been awake for hours but was trying not to disturb her roommate.

"Fine," Brianna croaked, her voice rough with sleep and the lingering effects of last night's alcohol. Her mouth tasted like copper and regret, her head pounding with each heartbeat. "What time is it?"

"Almost eleven. I was starting to worry, but figured you needed the sleep."

Eleven. On a Saturday. Which meant tomorrow would be Sunday, which meant churches across the country would fill with families like hers used to be—mothers and daughters sharing hymnals, fathers checking their phones during the sermon, teenagers texting under their bulletins while pretending to pay attention. All of them participating in the weekly ritual of pretending God was good, that prayers mattered, that showing up and singing the right songs could somehow protect you from the kind of loss that hollowed you out from the inside.

The thought made her stomach churn, though that might have been the hangover.

"I brought you water," Maya said, nodding toward Brianna's nightstand where a glass sat next to two aspirin. "And there's coffee if you want it."

The kindness was gentle, undemanding, but it still felt like pressure against her raw nerves. Brianna sat up carefully, the room spinning slightly, and reached for the water. The aspirin dissolved bitter on her tongue, chased by water that tasted like salvation she didn't deserve.

"Thanks," she managed.

Maya nodded and turned back to her textbook, but Brianna could feel her roommate's attention like a weight. Not judgmental, exactly, but present in a way that made her skin itch. Like Maya was cataloging details—the way Brianna's hands shook slightly, the mascara smudged under her eyes, the careful way she moved to avoid jarring her aching head.

Her phone buzzed against her leg, and Brianna fumbled for it with fingers that felt thick and uncoordinated. A text from her father, sent twenty minutes ago: Hope you're having a good weekend, kiddo. Thinking about you. Love, Dad.

The words were careful, deliberately casual, but Brianna could read the subtext. Tomorrow was Sunday. Her first Sunday away from home since the funeral. He was probably sitting in their kitchen right now, staring at the empty chair where her mother used to plan the week ahead over coffee and the church bulletin, trying to figure out how to fill the silence that had taken up residence in their house like an unwelcome guest.

"Another buzz. This time from Liam: Last night was incredible. I've been thinking about you all morning. Coffee in an hour? I know this perfect place."

The contrast between the messages was stark—her father's careful grief versus Liam's easy confidence. One represented everything she was running from; the other, everything she was running toward. The choice should have been simple.

So why did her thumb hover over her father's message instead of Liam's?

"Everything okay?" Maya asked again, and this time there was something different in her voice. Not just concern, but recognition. Like she'd seen this exact expression on someone else's face before.

"Just my dad checking in." Brianna set the phone aside without responding to either message. "He does that now. Since..."

She didn't finish the sentence, but Maya nodded anyway. "My uncle went through that after my aunt died. Suddenly he was calling everyone all the time, like he was afraid we'd disappear too if he didn't keep checking."

The casual mention of death, the acknowledgment that Maya understood something about loss, caught Brianna off guard. She'd assumed her roommate's relentless optimism came from a place of inexperience, that her faith was built on the foundation of a life where prayers got answered and good people didn't get sick.

"How long ago?" Brianna asked.

"Two years. Cancer." Maya's voice was matter-of-fact, but her fingers tightened around her coffee mug. "She was basically my second mom—lived with us after my parents divorced, helped raise me and my sister. The last six months were..." She paused, staring into her coffee. "I used to pray for miracles. Then I started praying for her pain to stop. When she died, I wasn't sure if I was relieved or devastated." Her laugh was soft and hollow. "Turns out you can be both."

Maya set down her mug carefully, as if it might shatter. "She taught me that choosing hope isn't about pretending everything's fine. It's about deciding that broken things can still hold light."

The information rearranged everything Brianna thought she knew about her roommate. Maya's careful kindness, her gentle persistence, the way she seemed to know exactly when to push and when to give space—it wasn't naive optimism. It was hard-won wisdom, forged in hospital rooms and sleepless nights, in the terrible mathematics of grief. Maya's brightness wasn't ignorance; it was defiance.

"I'm sorry," Brianna said, the words feeling inadequate but necessary.

"Thanks. It was... hard. Really hard. For a while, I thought I might lose my faith entirely." Maya glanced over, her expression carefully neutral. "Turns out anger and faith aren't mutually exclusive. Who knew?"

The words hung in the air between them, weighted with invitation. Brianna could feel Maya offering her something—not advice or platitudes, but simple recognition that doubt and rage could coexist with belief, that losing someone didn't automatically mean losing God.

But accepting that possibility meant admitting that her anger might not be the clean, righteous thing she'd convinced herself it was. It might just be grief wearing a different mask.

"I don't think I'm ready for that conversation yet," Brianna said quietly.

Maya nodded, turning back to her textbook. "That's okay. The conversation will be there when you are."

Brianna's phone buzzed again—Liam, probably wondering why she hadn't responded. She should text him back, make plans, continue building the new life she'd started last night. But something about Maya's casual revelation had shifted the air in their room, made the bright certainty of rebellion feel suddenly complicated.

Instead, she found herself asking, "What are you doing today?"

"Studying, mostly. I have a paper due Monday that I've been putting off." Maya gestured at the books scattered across her desk. "Nothing exciting. What about you?"

"I don't know. Maybe meet up with Liam."

"The guy from last night?"

"Yeah." Brianna waited for judgment, for some subtle indication that Maya disapproved of her choices. Instead, her roommate just nodded.

"He seems important to you."

It wasn't quite a question, but it felt like one anyway. Brianna considered how to answer. Important felt too strong—she'd known Liam for all of two days. But he represented something crucial: proof that she could build an identity separate from her grief, that she could be someone other than the girl whose mother died.

"He gets it," she said finally. "The anger, I mean. He doesn't try to fix it or explain it away."

"That's valuable," Maya said, and her tone was genuinely thoughtful. "Sometimes you need people who can sit in the dark with you."

"Exactly."

But even as she said it, Brianna found herself thinking about the way Liam had kissed her last night—hungry and possessive, like her pain was something he could consume. The memory made her skin prickle with unease she didn't want to examine too closely.

Her phone buzzed a third time. This time it was a group text from her old youth group: Missing you at our college send-off breakfast! Praying for your first semester!

The responses poured in like a flood of saccharine poison:

Madison: God has such amazing plans for you! Trust His timing!

Tyler: Can't wait to hear testimony about how the Lord is using this season to grow you!

Jess: Remember Jeremiah 29:11 - He knows the plans He has for you! Plans to prosper and not to harm!

Chloe: Can't wait to hear about all the ways God is working in your life! I just KNOW He's going to do something beautiful through your story!

Pastor Mike: Brianna, praying that you'll see His hand moving even in the hard times. Romans 8:28 - ALL things work together for good!

Each message landed like a physical blow. She could picture them perfectly—gathered around a table at IHOP, sharing updates about their new dorms and meal plans, their faces bright with the particular joy of young people whose faith had never been tested by anything worse than a failed exam or a summer camp crush. They spoke of God's goodness with the casual confidence of those who had never watched Him fail to answer the prayers that mattered most. Their assumption that He was "working" in her life—that her mother's death was somehow part of His beautiful plan—felt like being slapped by velvet gloves.

She deleted the entire thread without responding, her thumb trembling as she swiped away their well-meaning cruelty.

The casual assumption that God was working in her life—that her mother's death was somehow part of a divine plan rather than a cosmic cruelty—made her stomach churn with renewed force. These were the people who would tell her that her mother was "in a better place now," that her suffering had a purpose, that she should be grateful for the "growth" this experience would bring.

The thought of facing their bright certainty, their unshakeable belief that everything happened for a reason, made her want to crawl back under her covers and hide until the world made sense again.

Which, at this rate, might be never.

"You look like you've seen a ghost," Maya observed.

"Just some people from home." Brianna set her phone face-down on her nightstand, but she could still feel it there, a tiny rectangle of judgment and expectation. "They want to pray for me."

Maya's expression grew thoughtful. "And that bothers you?"

"It feels..." Brianna searched for words that wouldn't sound ungrateful. "Like they think prayer is some kind of magic spell. Like if they just say the right words, everything will be okay again."

"Maybe they're not trying to fix you," Maya said gently. "Maybe they just don't know what to do with feeling so helpless, you know?"

The suggestion caught Brianna off guard. She'd been so focused on her own pain that she hadn't considered that her friends might be struggling too—not with loss, but with the terrible recognition that bad things happened to good people, that faith wasn't a shield against suffering.

But acknowledging their pain meant acknowledging that they cared about her, which meant acknowledging that pushing them away was hurting people who'd done nothing wrong except fail to save her mother through the power of positive thinking.

The complexity of it all made her head pound worse.

"I need coffee," she said, standing carefully. "And a shower. And maybe to pretend it's not almost Sunday."

Maya's smile was small but understanding. "Sundays are hard. Even when you're not ready to admit why."

The observation was too accurate, too gentle, and Brianna felt something crack open in her chest—just a hairline fracture, but enough to let in a sliver of the warmth she'd been trying so hard to keep out.

"Yeah," she said quietly. "They are."

***

In the shower, standing under water hot enough to scald, Brianna let herself remember what Sundays used to mean. The steam rose around her like incense as she finally unlocked the door she'd kept bolted shut for eight months.

Not just church, but the whole ritual of it—her mother making pancakes while humming "How Great Thou Art" under her breath, the spatula scraping against the cast iron pan in perfect rhythm with the hymn. The smell of vanilla and cinnamon would drift upstairs, mixing with her father's aftershave and the particular scent of Sunday morning sunshine streaming through their kitchen windows. She could feel it now, the way her mother's flour-dusted fingers would brush her cheek when checking if she'd washed behind her ears, the gentle tug as those same hands braided her hair with the yellow ribbon that matched her dress.

Her father reading the paper and complaining good-naturedly about Pastor Williams' tendency toward long sermons, the rustle of newsprint and the clink of his coffee cup against the saucer—always the good china on Sundays, the set with tiny blue roses that her mother had inherited from Grandma Mae. The comfortable chaos of getting ready together, her mother's lipstick leaving coral crescents on coffee cup rims, her father's tie hanging loose around his collar until the very last minute when her mother would stand on tiptoe to knot it properly, her small hands smoothing the fabric down his chest.

After church, they'd go to lunch at Morrison's Diner where the vinyl booths were cracked and patched with silver tape, where her mother always ordered the same thing—grilled cheese cut diagonally, the way Brianna liked it, and tomato soup that she'd blow on delicately before each spoonful. Her father would steal fries off both their plates while pretending to be interested in his Greek salad, and her mother would swat his hand away with mock indignation, but she'd always push her plate closer to his reach. The jukebox would play Patsy Cline, and sometimes her parents would hum along, their voices blending in harmonies worn smooth by twenty years of marriage.

Then home for naps and homework and the particular kind of peace that came from knowing you belonged somewhere, that you were part of something larger than yourself. Her mother's hand stroking her hair as she dozed on the couch, the whisper of pages turning as her father worked the crossword puzzle, the tick of the grandfather clock in the hallway marking time that felt infinite and precious and utterly, completely safe.

The water turned cold against her skin, but Brianna couldn't move, couldn't breathe around the crushing weight of never again. Never again the flour-dusted fingers or the coral lipstick crescents or the gentle humming of hymns. Never again the Sunday morning sunshine or the yellow ribbon or the way her mother's voice would call up the stairs, "Breakfast, baby girl, before it gets cold." The sobs came then, raw and broken, echoing off the shower tiles like a prayer with no answer.

The memory was so vivid it took her breath away. Her mother's laugh echoing off the diner's tile walls. Her father's hand warm on her shoulder as they walked to the car. The absolute certainty that they would do this again next week, and the week after that, and every week until the end of time.

Brianna pressed her forehead against the cold shower tiles, the porcelain shock against her skin finally breaking the dam she'd built inside her chest. The sobs came in violent waves—not the bitter, surface tears that had sustained her through months of numbness, but something ancient and raw, torn from the hollowed-out cathedral where her faith used to echo. Her shoulders shook against the wall as she wept for those sacred Sunday mornings: the smell of her mother's coffee brewing at dawn, the worn hymnal pages they'd shared, the quiet benediction of fingers braiding her hair before church. She cried for the girl who had knelt beside her bed each night, whispering secrets to a God who listened, and for her mother's final breath—released in the terrible certainty that her daughter's prayers would carry her through whatever darkness waited beyond goodbye.

When she finally emerged from the bathroom, Maya was gone—probably at the library, or maybe at The Well for whatever Saturday activities they did there. A note on Brianna's desk read: Went to study. Text if you need anything. There's leftover pizza in the mini-fridge.

The kindness was small, practical, undemanding. Exactly what she needed without having to ask for it.

"Brianna picked up her phone and scrolled through her messages. Liam had texted twice more since this morning—first asking why she hadn't responded to his good morning text, then twenty minutes later wondering if everything was okay because she "usually replied by now." His tone had shifted from casual concern to something that felt heavier, more demanding of her attention. Her father's message still waited for a response. The youth group chat had accumulated three more messages, each one more aggressively cheerful than the last."

Instead of responding to any of them, she found herself opening a new message to Maya: Thanks for the pizza. And for understanding about Sundays.

The response came back almost immediately: Understanding is free. So is leftover pizza.

Something about the simple exchange—the lack of pressure, the gentle humor, the heart emoji that felt genuine rather than performative—made Brianna's chest tight with an emotion she couldn't name. It wasn't quite hope, but it wasn't despair either. Something in between, something that felt like the possibility of not being alone with her anger forever.

She spent the rest of the day in a strange liminal space—not quite ready to respond to Liam's increasingly frequent texts, but not ready to ignore them either. Not willing to call her father back, but not able to delete his message. Caught between the girl she'd been and the person she was trying to become, with no clear path forward.

As evening approached and Sunday loomed closer, Brianna found herself thinking about what Maya had said: that anger and faith weren't mutually exclusive. The idea felt dangerous, like a crack in the wall she'd built around her heart. Because if she could be angry at God and still believe in him, then what excuse did she have for cutting herself off from everything that had once brought her comfort?

If faith could survive fury, then maybe she didn't have to choose between loving her mother and hating the God who'd taken her away.

But that was a thought for another day, another version of herself. Tonight, she had to get through the long hours until Monday, when she could lose herself in classes and the comfortable routine of being a college student instead of a daughter learning how to grieve.

Her phone buzzed one more time—Liam again, asking if she was okay. This time, she typed back: Sorry, family stuff. Talk tomorrow?

His response was immediate: Of course. Sweet dreams.

The casualness of it should have been comforting, but instead it felt hollow. Like he was playing a role rather than actually caring about her answer. Or maybe that was just her own guilt talking, the part of her that knew she was using him as a shield against feelings too complicated to face.

Either way, tomorrow she would have to decide who she was going to be—the girl who kissed boys at parties and fed herself on fury alone, or someone large enough to contain contradictions. Someone who could cradle both rage and tenderness, doubt and faith, the radical notion that healing might mean remembering differently rather than not at all.

For now, she smoothed Maya's note against her palm like a prayer she was learning to believe in, testing the weight of kindness that asked for nothing in return—as constant and unlikely as Sunday morning light streaming through her bedroom window, illuminating dust motes that danced whether she watched them or not.

Outside their window, Saturday night settled over campus like a blanket, muffling the sounds of students living their uncomplicated lives. Tomorrow would be Sunday, and the day after that would be Monday, and somehow she would figure out how to keep breathing through all of them.

It wasn't much of a plan, but it was enough for now.

Chapter Five

An Essay as a Weapon

The cursor blinked like a metronome of accusation against the white void of her laptop screen, its pulse syncing with the throb of blood vessels behind Brianna's swollen eyes. Her shoulders hunched forward, vertebrae grinding against each other as grief crystallized into something sharper, more dangerous. The assignment prompt glowed beneath that merciless cursor—analyze Hopkins' treatment of mortality—and her fingers trembled above the keys, knuckles white with the effort of restraint. Her jaw ached from clenching, molars ground together until her skull felt ready to crack. The cursor blinked again, waiting, hungry for the violence she was about to unleash.

Around her, Dr. Finch's classroom hummed with the particular energy of students pretending to pay attention—the scratch of pens on paper, the soft tap of fingers on keyboards, the rustle of pages being turned with studied thoughtfulness. Someone behind her was breathing through their mouth, a wet, rhythmic sound that made her want to scream.

She'd been staring at the assignment on the screen, for twenty minutes: "Write a critical analysis of Gerard Manley Hopkins' 'Terrible Sonnets,' examining the relationship between faith and doubt in his darkest period. Consider how Hopkins wrestles with God's silence while maintaining his devotion. 3-5 pages, due Friday."

The words swam on the screen, each one a small provocation. *Faith and doubt. God's silence. Maintaining devotion.* It was as if Dr. Finch had reached directly into her chest and pulled out the exact wound he wanted her to dissect in public.

Around her, her classmates scribbled notes about Hopkins' "spiritual crisis" and his "ultimate reconciliation with divine love." She could hear fragments of their whispered conversations: "It's so beautiful how he finds God even in his despair..." "The way he surrenders to mystery is so profound..." "His faith is actually stronger because of the doubt..."

The familiar rage built in her chest, clean and sharp as a blade being forged. These people—these children—speaking about divine abandonment like it was an intellectual exercise, a literary device to be analyzed and admired. None of them had knelt beside a hospital bed, begging a silent God to perform one small miracle. None of them had watched faith crumble like ash in their hands while everyone around them insisted it was somehow beautiful.

Her fingers attacked the keyboard with savage precision, each keystroke a small act of violence against months of swallowed humiliation. The words didn't just come—they erupted, pouring out in torrents as her rage finally found its voice. Her hands moved with barely-controlled fury, fingers hammering the keys so hard the laptop trembled beneath the assault. This wasn't writing; this was releasing—months of suppressed pain transformed into weapons disguised as academic prose, each sentence a carefully sharpened blade aimed directly at Hopkins' throat.

The Comfortable Lie of Hopkins' "Terrible Sonnets"

A Critical Analysis by Brianna Matthews

Gerard Manley Hopkins' so-called "Terrible Sonnets" represent not a profound spiritual journey, but a masterclass in intellectual self-deception. Hopkins, writing from the privileged position of a Jesuit priest with a guaranteed roof over his head and a community of believers to validate his struggles, crafts what amounts to spiritual theater—a performance of doubt designed to ultimately reinforce rather than challenge his faith.

Consider the fundamental dishonesty of "Carrion Comfort": "Not, I'll not, carrion comfort, Despair, not feast on thee." Hopkins rejects despair not because he has found genuine reason for hope, but because his institutional framework demands it. This is not faith wrestling with honest doubt; it is dogma wearing the costume of struggle. True despair—the kind that comes from watching a loving God remain silent while good people suffer—doesn't politely step aside when we refuse to "feast" on it. It devours us anyway.

The poem continues: "Not untwist—slack they may be—these last strands of man. In me or, most weary, cry I can no more." Here, Hopkins reveals the essential cowardice of his position. He clings to "last strands" of faith not because they offer genuine comfort or truth, but because the alternative—true acknowledgment of divine absence—is too terrifying to contemplate. His "I can no more" is not an honest surrender to reality but a theatrical gesture, safe in the knowledge that his religious community will interpret his doubt as spiritual depth rather than intellectual honesty.

The most insidious aspect of Hopkins' work is how it has been canonized by literary scholars and religious institutions as an example of "faith through darkness." This interpretation requires us to ignore the fundamental question: What if the darkness is not a temporary testing ground but simply the truth? What if God's silence is not mysterious divine pedagogy but evidence of absence? Hopkins never seriously considers these possibilities because his career, his identity, and his social position depend on not considering them.

In "No worst, there is none," Hopkins writes: "O the mind, mind has mountains; cliffs of fall / Frightful, sheer, no-man-fathomed." This metaphor of psychological landscape as treacherous terrain is striking, but it serves to mystify rather than clarify. By making suffering into poetry, Hopkins domesticates it, makes it serve his theological agenda. Real grief—the kind that follows you into grocery stores and makes you forget how to sleep—doesn't arrange itself into neat metaphors. It doesn't provide material for beautiful, quotable lines about the soul's geography.

The final lines of this sonnet are perhaps the most telling: "Here! creep, / Wretch, under a comfort serves in a whirlwind: all / Life death does end and each day dies with sleep." Hopkins finds comfort in the promise of ending, in the daily mercy of unconsciousness. But notice how even this surrender is framed within the context of divine provision—comfort "serves" in the whirlwind, as if God is still somehow orchestrating even the temporary relief of sleep. This is not honest engagement with meaninglessness; it is the desperate reframing of abandonment as mysterious love.

Hopkins' reputation as a poet of "honest doubt" reveals more about our culture's need for sanitized suffering than it does about the quality of his spiritual insights. We celebrate his "Terrible Sonnets" because they offer us a model of how to suffer beautifully, how to transform genuine anguish into art that ultimately serves institutional purposes. They provide a template for making pain productive, for finding meaning in meaninglessness—in short, for lying to ourselves about the brutal randomness of existence.

True spiritual honesty would look different. It would acknowledge that some prayers go unanswered not because God has a better plan, but because there is no God to answer them. It would recognize that some suffering teaches us nothing except that the universe is indifferent to human pain. It would resist the urge to find silver linings, deeper meanings, or hidden blessings in experiences that are simply, irreducibly terrible.

Hopkins' "Terrible Sonnets" are terrible in all the wrong ways—not because they confront genuine spiritual darkness, but because they illuminate how even our most celebrated expressions of doubt can become sophisticated forms of denial. They show us what it looks like when institutional faith co-opts the language of despair for its own purposes, transforming honest questions into rhetorical devices that ultimately serve to silence rather than answer them.

In the end, Hopkins gives us not the comfort of truth, but the more seductive comfort of beautiful lies. And perhaps that is the most terrible thing of all.

Brianna's fingers stilled on the keyboard, her heart hammering against her ribs. The essay felt like a confession and a battle cry all at once. Every word was true, every argument earned through nights spent staring at the ceiling, through months of watching well-meaning people try to explain away the inexplicable. This wasn't an academic exercise. This was her manifesto.

She read through it once, then again, each pass only strengthening her conviction. Let Dr. Finch read this. Let him try to gentle-shepherd his way through her logic. Let him attempt to find the "hurt little girl" beneath her intellectual armor. She had built this argument like a fortress, and she dared anyone to try to tear it down.

The class period ended, students gathering their things and filing out in the usual post-lecture shuffle. Brianna saved her document, closed her laptop with a decisive snap, and walked to the front of the room where Dr. Finch was erasing the whiteboard.

"I have my essay," she said, her voice steady.

He turned, his expression mildly curious. "Already? I only assigned it yesterday."

"I work better when the material is fresh," she said, extending a printed copy. She'd made sure to use the good printer in the library, the one that produced crisp, professional pages. Even the formatting was armor—12-point Times New Roman, perfectly justified margins, her arguments marching down the page in orderly battalions.

Dr. Finch accepted the paper, his eyes scanning the title. His eyebrows rose slightly, but his expression remained neutral. "Ambitious thesis," he said quietly.

"I believe in intellectual honesty," Brianna replied, the words carrying just enough edge to make her position clear. This wasn't a student seeking approval. This was a scholar demanding to be taken seriously.

"I can see that." He glanced up at her, those perceptive eyes taking in her defensive posture, the slight lift of her chin, the way her hands were clenched at her sides. "I'll read this carefully and have some thoughts for you by Monday. Are you free during office hours?"

The invitation felt like a challenge being issued from across a battlefield. "Tuesday at three," she said.

"Tuesday at three," he confirmed. "I look forward to our discussion."

As she walked out of the classroom, Brianna felt the particular satisfaction that came from firing the first shot in a war she intended to win. Dr. Finch could read her essay with all the gentle understanding he wanted. He could prepare his soft questions and his knowing looks. But she had given him something he couldn't dismiss, couldn't therapeutize, couldn't reduce to mere symptoms of grief.

She had given him her mind, sharp and unyielding as a blade.

Let him try to find the broken little girl now.

Maya was at her desk when Brianna returned to their room, surrounded by her usual explosion of color-coded notes and cheerful chaos. She looked up as the door opened, her expression brightening with the automatic warmth that had once annoyed Brianna so much.

"Hey, how was Finch's class?" Maya asked, spinning around in her chair. "I heard he assigned the Hopkins essay. Are you going to write about the 'Terrible Sonnets'? I loved those when I read them in high school. So raw and honest about struggling with faith."

The casual mention of the poems made Brianna's jaw clench. Of course Maya had loved them. Of course she'd found them "honest" and "raw." Maya, with her fairy lights and her unshakeable optimism, would naturally gravitate toward poetry that made doubt look beautiful, that transformed spiritual struggle into inspiration.

"I wrote about them," Brianna said, her voice carefully neutral.

"Oh cool! What angle did you take?" Maya's genuine interest was clear, her face open and expectant. She leaned forward slightly, setting down her highlighter—she'd been color-coding her sociology notes with the kind of methodical care she brought to everything. There was something in Brianna's tone, though, something too carefully neutral, that made Maya tilt her head just a fraction. "I bet you found something really unique to explore."

For a moment, Brianna considered telling her. Explaining how Hopkins' sonnets were elaborate lies, how faith and doubt weren't mysterious dance partners but simply incompatible worldviews, how the entire literary establishment had been taken in by pretty words disguising ugly truths.

But looking at Maya's bright, curious expression, Brianna realized it would be like trying to explain the weight of shadows to someone who had only ever lived in sunlight.

Maya existed in a world where suffering had meaning, where questions led to answers, where God's silence was somehow still a form of communication. There was no bridge between that world and the stark landscape Brianna had mapped in her essay.

"Just a critical analysis," she said finally. "Looking at the relationship between faith and doubt."

"That sounds fascinating," Maya said, turning back to her textbook. "I'd love to read it sometime if you don't mind sharing."

Brianna made a noncommittal noise and sat on her bed, pulling out her phone. There was a text from Liam: *How did the academic sheep take your intellectual superiority today?*

She found herself smiling for the first time since morning. *Delivered my Hopkins essay to Finch. Tore apart his precious "Terrible Sonnets."*

His response was immediate: *My brilliant iconoclast. You've done it again—another surgical strike against their comfortable mediocrity. Dinner at The Alibi to toast your latest act of literary terrorism? I need to hear every detail of how you dismantled their precious assumptions.*

Yes, she typed back. *I need to decompress with someone who actually thinks.*

As she gathered her things for dinner, Brianna caught sight of herself in the small mirror above her desk. The girl looking back at her was sharp-eyed and fierce, her mouth set in a line of determined satisfaction. This was what intellectual courage looked like. This was what it meant to refuse the comfortable lies that kept most people docile and deluded.

She had spent months building walls against the world's attempts to comfort her, to explain away her pain, to find meaning in meaninglessness.

Today, she had finally gone on the offensive. She had taken her rage and shaped it into something precise and deadly, an argument that couldn't be dismissed or diminished.

Tomorrow, Dr. Finch would read her essay and realize he was facing not a grieving student in need of gentle guidance, but an intellectual equal who refused to accept his worldview. The battle lines were drawn.

And Brianna was ready for war.

The evening at The Alibi unfolded exactly as she'd hoped. Liam read her essay on his phone, his expression growing more appreciative with each paragraph—but there was something calculating in the way he paused at certain lines, his lips curving into a smile that felt less about her achievement and more about vindication.

"This is exactly what I've been trying to tell people," he said, handing back her phone with the reverence of someone discovering a particularly sharp weapon. "You've articulated the brutality of it all so perfectly. The way you dissect the illusion of progress, the false hope they peddle—" He leaned back in his chair, eyes gleaming with the satisfaction of finding an intellectual ally. "Most people are too comfortable in their delusions to see what you see. But this," he gestured at her screen, "this cuts right through their naive optimism."

She felt a flush of pride, but something nagged at her—the way he kept saying 'they' and 'people,' as if her personal anguish had become evidence in his case against the world. As if her pain was valuable to him not because it was hers, but because it proved him right.

When he finished, he looked up at her with something approaching awe.

"This is brilliant," he said, his voice low and intense. "You've taken apart not just Hopkins, but the entire academic-industrial complex that profits from packaging doubt as devotion. You've exposed the whole charade."

The validation was intoxicating. Here was someone who understood not just her arguments but the courage it had taken to make them. Someone who recognized that her essay wasn't just about poetry—it was about refusing to let beautiful language obscure ugly truths.

"I'm tired of pretending," she said, the beer making her bolder, more articulate. "Tired of watching people worship their own delusions and calling it profound."

"That's exactly what Hopkins was doing," Liam agreed. "And what Finch is doing by teaching him as some kind of spiritual guide. They're pushing a drug—the opiate of manufactured meaning—and calling it medicine."

They talked late into the night, deconstructing not just Hopkins but the entire pantheon of writers who had dared to find hope in hopeless situations. Emily Dickinson's slant of light became self-deception. T.S. Eliot's still point was escapism. Every poem that suggested suffering might lead to wisdom was revealed as propaganda for a worldview that couldn't survive honest scrutiny.

Walking back to campus under the indifferent stars, Brianna felt the particular satisfaction of a day well-fought. She had refused to be broken by her grief, refused to be gentle-shepherded into acceptance, refused to transform her mother's death into material for someone else's theology.

She had taken her pain and forged it into a weapon.

And on Tuesday, she would find out how sharp its edge really was.

Tuesday afternoon arrived with the weight of an execution date.

Brianna stood outside Dr. Finch's office, her printed essay clutched in one hand like evidence in her own defense, though she couldn't decide if she was the prosecutor or the defendant. The hallway smelled of old books and floor wax, institutional scents that reminded her of church basements and youth group meetings—spaces where authority figures had once smiled at her with the same gentle patience she was about to face.

Through the frosted glass of his door, she could see Dr. Finch's silhouette bent over papers at his desk. Her essay, most likely. The hallway stretched behind her, lined with identical office doors and fluorescent lights that hummed with an electric persistence. The scent of old books and industrial disinfectant clung to the air—that particular academic cocktail that usually comforted her but now seemed stifling.

Brianna shifted her weight from one foot to the other, the stack of printed emails and drafts growing heavier in her sweaty palms despite their negligible weight. She'd rehearsed this confrontation a dozen times in her dorm room mirror, had armed herself with citations and evidence, had built her argument like the fortress of logic it was. But her body refused to cooperate—her heart hammered against her ribs, and she could feel a bead of perspiration trailing down her spine beneath her carefully chosen blazer. Somewhere down the hall, a door creaked open and clicked shut, footsteps echoing briefly before fading. The mundane sound made her flinch.

She imagined him reading her carefully constructed arguments, his pen poised to make notes in the margins—not corrections, but observations. The kind of thoughtful, probing comments that professors made when they saw through your intellectual armor to the wounded animal underneath.

The thought made her stomach clench with something that wasn't quite fear but wasn't confidence either. She had spent two days replaying their coming conversation, scripting responses to his inevitable attempts to psychoanalyze her thesis. He would probably start with something gentle: "This is powerful writing, Brianna, but I sense there's more going on here than literary criticism." Then would come the soft questions, the tilted head, the invitation to share what was "really" bothering her.

She was ready for all of it. Her arguments were solid, her logic unassailable. She had done her research, built her case brick by brick. If Dr. Finch wanted to engage with her ideas rather than her psychology, she would destroy him with facts. If he chose to play therapist instead of teacher, she would expose that condescension for what it was.

Either way, she would win.

Brianna knocked twice, sharp raps that echoed down the empty hallway.

"Come in," came his voice, warm and unhurried.

She pushed open the door and stepped into the cramped sanctuary of his office. It looked exactly as she remembered—books stacked on every surface, papers graded and ungraded forming precarious towers, the window looking out onto the quad where students moved between classes in their predictable patterns. The air smelled of pipe tobacco and old paper, comforting scents that she refused to find comforting.

Dr. Finch looked up from his desk, his reading glasses perched on the end of his nose, and smiled. Not the patronizing smile she had braced herself for, but something smaller, more genuinely pleased.

"Brianna. Thank you for coming." He gestured to the chair across from his desk. "Please, sit."

She remained standing, her essay held against her chest like a shield. "I assume you've read it."

"I have." He leaned back in his chair, his fingers steepled beneath his chin. "Multiple times, actually. It's quite remarkable."

The word hung in the air between them, loaded with potential meanings. Remarkable could mean impressive. It could also mean concerning, unusual, worthy of closer examination. Brianna waited for the qualifier, the gentle but that would reveal his true assessment.

Instead, Dr. Finch reached across his desk and picked up her essay, the margins filled with his neat handwriting. But when he looked up at her, his expression wasn't one of concern or therapeutic interest. It was something else entirely—something that looked almost like respect.

"You've written a devastating critique," he said quietly. "Your argument is sophisticated, your analysis is thorough, and your conclusions follow logically from your premises. As a piece of literary criticism, it's quite accomplished."

Brianna felt a flutter of confusion. This wasn't how she'd expected him to begin. Where was the gentle probing? The attempt to redirect her anger toward more "productive" channels?

"Thank you," she said, though the words came out stiffer than she intended.

"I gave you an A," Dr. Finch continued, turning the essay so she could see the grade written in red ink at the top. "Your scholarship is impeccable. Your prose is clear and forceful. You've successfully dismantled Hopkins' reputation as a poet of honest doubt and revealed the institutional machinery that sustains certain interpretations of his work."

He set the paper down and removed his reading glasses, cleaning them with a soft cloth he pulled from his desk drawer. The gesture was unhurried, almost meditative.

"But I have to ask," he said, looking up at her with those perceptive eyes that seemed to see too much, "what do you plan to do with all that anger?"

There it was. The question she had been dreading and preparing for. But something about the way he asked it—not as a therapist diagnosing a patient, but as one scholar asking another about their research methodology—caught her off guard.

"I don't know what you mean," she said, though they both knew it was a lie.

Dr. Finch put his glasses back on and leaned forward slightly, his elbows resting on the desk. "Hopkins wrote his 'Terrible Sonnets' during what scholars call his period of spiritual desolation. He was isolated, depressed, struggling with his faith and his calling. The poems emerged from a place of genuine anguish—the kind that makes you question everything you once believed."

Brianna's jaw tightened. "I covered that in my essay. His anguish was real, but his response to it was intellectually dishonest. He refused to follow his doubts to their logical conclusion."

"Perhaps," Dr. Finch said. "Or perhaps he was working through his doubts in the only way he knew how—through language, through craft, through the attempt to make meaning from meaninglessness." He paused, his gaze steady on her face. "The way you're doing now."

The comparison hit like a physical blow. "I'm not doing what Hopkins did. I'm not trying to preserve faith in the face of contrary evidence. I'm following the evidence wherever it leads, even if—especially if—it leads to conclusions that make people uncomfortable."

"I don't doubt your intellectual courage," Dr. Finch said gently. "But I wonder if you've considered that your essay isn't actually about Hopkins at all."

Brianna felt heat rise in her chest, the familiar surge of defensive anger. "Of course it's about Hopkins. I spent pages analyzing his work, his his-torical context, his—"

"Your essay," Dr. Finch interrupted softly, "is about a young woman who prayed for a miracle and didn't receive one. It's about someone who trusted in a loving God and felt abandoned when she needed divine intervention most. It's about the rage that comes from discovering that the adults who taught you about faith might have been wrong about its power to protect the people you love."

Each word landed with surgical precision, cutting through her carefully constructed arguments to the raw wound beneath. Brianna's hands shook slightly, but she forced her voice to remain steady.

"You're psychologizing my work instead of engaging with my arguments. That's exactly the kind of intellectual dishonesty I wrote about."

"Am I?" Dr. Finch reached for a book on his desk—a worn copy of Hopkins' collected poems—and opened it to a page marked with a yellow sticky note. "Let me read you something. From 'No worst, there is none': 'Comforter, where, where is your comforting? Mary, mother of us, where is your relief?'"

He looked up at her. "Hopkins is asking the same question you're asking, Brianna. Where is the comfort that was promised? Where is the relief that faith was supposed to provide? The difference is that you've decided the absence of an answer proves the question itself was meaningless. Hopkins chose to wrestle with the silence."

"Wrestling with silence is just another way of talking to yourself," Brianna shot back. "It's a sophisticated form of self-deception."

"Maybe," Dr. Finch said. "Or maybe it's the most honest thing a human being can do when faced with the unexplainable. Maybe the wrestling is more important than winning."

Brianna stared at him, her essay clutched so tightly in her hands that her knuckles had gone white. He wasn't dismissing her arguments or trying to fix her pain. He was taking her seriously—too seriously, perhaps. He was treating her intellectual fury as worthy of engagement rather than symptoms to be soothed.

It was infuriating and deeply unsettling.

"I don't need to wrestle," she said, her voice harder now. "I need to face reality. My mother is dead. Prayer didn't save her. God either doesn't exist or doesn't care. Those are facts, not mysteries to be explored through poetry."

"Yes," Dr. Finch said simply. "Those are facts. Terrible, irreducible facts."

The agreement hit her like a physical blow. She had braced herself for pushback, for him to counter with alternative interpretations, to invoke God's mysterious ways, to offer some cushioning reframe that would dull the blade of her conclusion. Instead, his direct acknowledgment left her reeling, muscles still coiled for a fight that wasn't coming.

Instead, he just sat there, acknowledging the facts she had spent months forcing herself to accept. The absence of argument felt more destabilizing than any debate would have.

"Then what's the point?" she asked, and for the first time, her voice cracked slightly. "What's the point of wrestling with questions that have no answers? What's the point of making meaning from experiences that are just randomly, brutally meaningless?"

Dr. Finch was quiet for a long moment, his gaze moving to the window where late afternoon light was beginning to slant across the quad. When he spoke again, his voice was soft, almost reverent.

"After my son died, I spent two years trying to solve the equation of his loss. I read theology, philosophy, grief counseling books—*everything* I could get my hands on. I was looking for the answer that would make his death make sense, that would restore some order to a universe that had revealed itself to be fundamentally chaotic.

I know what it's like to sit in a hospital room and bargain with a God you're not even sure you believe in. I know the particular guilt that comes with being a parent—wondering if you missed some sign, if you should have pushed the doctors harder, if you somehow failed in the most fundamental way possible. I couldn't concentrate on my research for months. My colleagues kept telling me to take more time, but work was the only thing that kept me from drowning completely.

The questions you're asking yourself—*Why him? Why now? What was the point of any of it?*—I asked those same questions until they nearly drove me mad. I thought my training, my understanding of human psychology, would somehow insulate me from the worst of it. **But grief doesn't care about your degrees or your expertise.** It strips you down to nothing and forces you to rebuild yourself from scratch."

He turned back to her, and she saw something in his eyes she hadn't expected—not pity, but kinship. The recognition of someone who had walked the same desolate road.

"I never found that answer, Brianna. The equation doesn't solve. The universe doesn't become orderly or just or comprehensible. But in the wrestling, in the refusal to stop asking the questions even when you know there are no answers—in that, I found something else."

"What?" The word came out barely above a whisper.

"Company," he said simply. "The company of everyone who has ever loved someone enough to be broken by their loss. The company of poets like Hopkins, who chose to make art from anguish instead of letting the anguish win. The company of students like you, who care enough about truth to be furious when the world fails to provide it."

Tears pricked at the corners of Brianna's eyes, but she blinked them back fiercely. She would not cry in this office. She would not give him the satisfaction of seeing her break.

"That's not enough," she said.

"No," Dr. Finch agreed. "It's not. It's not enough at all. But it's what we have. And sometimes, what we have is more substantial than what we've lost—not because it fills the void, but because it acknowledges the void's reality while refusing to be consumed by it."

He reached across the desk and slid her essay back toward her. "Your anger is magnificent, Brianna. It's clean and honest and absolutely justified. But anger is a fuel, not a destination. The question isn't whether you should feel it—of course you should. The question is what you're going to build with it."

Brianna stared down at her essay, at the red A blazing at the top of the first page like a small victory flag. But the victory felt hollow now, incomplete. She had won the argument, but winning had revealed the inadequacy of argument itself.

"I don't know how to build anything," she admitted, the words barely audible.

"No one does, at first," Dr. Finch said. "But that's what makes it an act of faith—not faith in divine providence or cosmic justice, but faith in the possibility that meaning can be made rather than found. That love can be stronger than loss, even when loss has the last word."

He stood up, moving around the desk to lean against its edge, closer to her but not invasively so. "Hopkins wrote his 'Terrible Sonnets' not because he had found answers, but because he refused to stop asking questions. Your essay is its own kind of terrible sonnet, Brianna. It's a prayer disguised as an argument. A desperate conversation with a God you're not sure you believe in anymore."

The observation hit with the force of revelation, stealing her breath and sending a tremor through her hands. *Her essay*—this carefully constructed fortress of logic and reason that she had wielded like a sword against faith—suddenly transformed before her eyes. The words seemed to shimmer and rearrange themselves on the page, revealing their true nature. Not the confident manifesto of someone who had moved beyond belief, but something far more vulnerable: *prayer disguised as argument.*

The recognition was immediate and devastating. Every passionate rebuttal, every carefully marshaled piece of evidence, every moment she had spent crafting her case against God—it had all been one long, anguished conversation *with* Him. Her throat tightened as the truth settled into her bones: she hadn't been arguing against faith at all. She had been wrestling with it, the way Jacob wrestled with the angel, demanding answers, demanding to be heard. Her essay wasn't the work of someone who had found peace in disbelief—it was the desperate cry of someone still fighting for connection, still hoping to be found.

The armor she had spent years forging cracked wide open, leaving her exposed to a truth she had been running from all along.

"I can't," she whispered. "I can't keep wrestling. It hurts too much."

"I know," Dr. Finch said, and his voice carried the weight of his own losses, his own wrestling matches with the inexplicable. "But the alternative—the complete surrender of the questions—hurts more. It's a different kind of death, the death of the part of you that cares enough to demand answers."

Brianna looked up at him, this professor who had read her rage and reflected it back to her not as pathology but as love wearing different clothes. She thought of Liam, who would have praised her essay as a perfect example of intellectual clarity, who would have used it as further evidence of their shared superiority to the deluded masses.

But Dr. Finch saw something else in her words—not the end of faith, but faith's most honest expression. Not the absence of love, but love so fierce it refused to be comforted by lies.

"What do I do?" she asked, the question pulled from the deepest part of her, where the little girl who had once knelt beside her bed still lived, still hoping for someone to answer.

"You keep writing," Dr. Finch said simply. "You keep asking the hard questions. You keep making art from anguish, meaning from meaninglessness, beauty from the ruins of your beautiful certainties. You let the wrestling make you strong enough to help others who are wrestling too."

He moved back to his chair, giving her space to process what he'd said. "Your next essay assignment is open-ended—any poet, any theme, any approach you want to take. I'd be interested to see what you write when you're not trying to tear something down, but to build something up."

Brianna stood slowly, her legs unsteady beneath her. The armor she had worn into this office lay in pieces around her feet, but she didn't feel exposed. She felt... possible. Like someone who might, eventually, figure out how to live in a world that made no sense but demanded to be lived in anyway.

"Thank you," she said, meaning it in ways she couldn't fully articulate.

"Thank you," Dr. Finch replied, "for reminding me why I became a teacher. For showing me what honest doubt looks like. For wrestling with the text—and with me—instead of accepting easy answers."

As she gathered her things to leave, Brianna paused at the door. "Dr. Finch? The wrestling—does it ever get easier?"

He considered the question seriously, his expression thoughtful. "No," he said finally. "But you get stronger. And eventually, you discover that the wrestling itself is a kind of prayer. The most honest kind, perhaps."

Walking out of his office, Brianna felt lighter and heavier at the same time—lighter because she no longer had to carry the weight of absolute certainty, heavier because she now understood the responsibility that came with honest questioning. The hallway looked the same, but she moved through it differently, like someone who had discovered that the ground beneath her feet was both less solid and more substantial than she had ever imagined.

Her essay, tucked into her backpack with its bright red A, no longer felt like a weapon. It felt like the first page of a much longer story—one she was only beginning to learn how to tell.

Chapter Six

The Gospel of Nothing

The Alibi felt less like a choice and more like a necessity. After the sterile white box of Dr. Finch's office, with its quiet, threatening empathy that demanded to be let in, Brianna needed its opposite. She needed Liam's world. She craved the familiar welcome of a floor so sticky your shoes made a sound like tearing tape with every step. She needed the low-wattage amber gloom, a honeyed darkness that was kind not just to secrets, but to the ugly faces people made when they were hurting. The jukebox in the corner wasn't just weeping; it was hemorrhaging a song about a truck, a dog, and a broken heart, its bassline a thrum she could feel in her teeth.

The air, thick with the ghosts of last night's cigarettes and the hot, greasy promise of onion rings, was a comforting blanket that tasted of stale beer and shared apathy. This was a sanctuary built from peeling varnish and indifference. No one here would ever lean in with the gentle, probing questions that felt like scalpels in Dr. Finch's hands. Here, a haunted look was just the price of admission. Fury wasn't a symptom to be cured; it was the baseline.

Liam was already in their corner booth when she arrived, a pitcher of cheap beer sweating between his hands. He looked up as she approached, and his smile wasn't the easy, charming one from the involvement fair. It was sharper, more knowing. The smile of a co-conspirator.

"There she is," he said, pouring her a glass without asking. "The philosopher-warrior, returned from her parley with the enemy."

Brianna slid onto the cracked vinyl, the cool surface a welcome shock against her skin. "He gave me an A," she said, her voice flat.

"Of course he did. He's not a fool." Liam pushed a glass toward her. "But he didn't let it go at that, did he? He tried the gentle shepherd routine. The soft voice, the look of deep concern. Am I close?"

The accuracy was so startling it felt like he'd been in the room. The relief was immediate and overwhelming. She wasn't crazy. She hadn't imagined the subtle pressure, the quiet disassembly of her defenses.

"He said my anger came from a place of love," she admitted, the words tasting like a confession. "He said my essay wasn't an argument against God, but an argument *with* Him. That it was a prayer."

Liam let out a short, bitter laugh. "Oh, that's a classic. Masterful, even. See what he did there? He took your power—your intellectual clarity—and reframed it as a weakness. As a cry for help. He turned your weapon into a wound."

He leaned forward, his elbows resting on the carved-up table, his voice dropping to a low, intense murmur that cut through the bar's noise. "They can't stand an elegant, cohesive argument for despair, Brianna. It threatens their entire worldview, which is built on the flimsy promise that suffering has a purpose. So they can't engage with your ideas. Instead, they have to engage with your *pathology*. They have to make you the broken one."

Every word was a balm on the raw, confused wound Dr. Finch had left behind. Liam was rebuilding her fortress, handing her the bricks and mortar himself.

"He told me to be kind to myself," she whispered.

"The tyranny of other people's care," Liam said, nodding knowingly. "It sounds nice, doesn't it? 'Be kind to yourself.' But what he's really saying is, 'Your anger makes me uncomfortable. Soften it. Tame it. Make it palatable for me.' It's the most insidious form of control."

She took a long drink of the beer. It was bitter and cold, and it felt like truth. "How do you know all this?"

His expression darkened almost imperceptibly. "I told you about my father. The foreclosure lawyer deacon. For years, I tried to have these conversations with him. I'd bring him Kierkegaard, Nietzsche, Camus. I'd try to show him the logical inconsistencies, the moral hypocrisy. And you know what he'd do?" Liam looked down at his glass. "He'd put his hand on my shoulder and say, 'Son, I'm praying for your heart to soften.' He never once engaged with my mind. Because to him, my doubt wasn't an intellectual position. It was a spiritual sickness. A broken heart that needed Jesus to fix it."

The bitterness in his voice was so profound, so familiar, that it felt like her own. It was the anger of being fundamentally misunderstood, of having your mind dismissed in favor of your perceived emotional fragility.

"Of course he'd call it that." Liam's voice was soft, dangerously reasonable, as if he were validating a child's fear of the dark. He didn't dismiss the idea; he enveloped it. "The entire system is designed to create that feeling in you, Brianna. Dr. Finch's role is to help you adapt to the cage. A perfectly noble goal. But he'll never encourage you to see the bars. "His passion began to rise, not in volume, but in a focused, intellectual intensity. "That's what hope is. It isn't a virtue. It's a sophisticated instrument of social control. They pathologize your clarity as cynicism, then they sell you hope as the cure. It's the leash the universe uses to keep you coming back for more punishment. Think about it: 'It's all part of God's plan.' 'He'll never give you more than you can handle.' 'What doesn't kill you makes you stronger.' It's all just propaganda designed to make you accept unbearable pain without fighting back."

"So what's the alternative?" she asked, though she already knew the answer. She just needed to hear him say it.

"The Gospel of Nothing," he said, his eyes locking with hers. "And it's not an empty gospel. It's the most liberating one there is. It means you can stop searching for meaning in the wreckage. Your mom's death wasn't a test. It wasn't a lesson. It wasn't part of some grand, cosmic plan. It was a random, meaningless, statistical tragedy. It was biology doing what biology does. And it was freaking awful."

He said the last words with such simple, unvarnished finality that something inside Brianna finally, blessedly, broke loose. He wasn't trying to make it better. He wasn't trying to find a silver lining. He was just sitting with her in the brutal, ugly truth of it.

"And if it was meaningless," he went on, his voice softer now, "then you're free. You don't owe her memory some performance of perfect grief. You don't owe God your anger or your forgiveness. You don't owe anyone a happy ending. You are completely, terrifyingly, beautifully free to just be a person who had something terrible happen to her, and who is figuring out how to keep breathing."

Tears pricked at the corners of her eyes, but they weren't the hot, messy tears of Saturday's shower. They were tears of profound, aching relief. He was giving her permission to lay down the crushing weight of having to make it all *mean* something.

He reached across the table, his fingers brushing against hers. His touch was warm and real against the cold, sweating glass. "Your anger is the most honest thing you have right now, Brianna. It's a sign that you're still alive, that you're refusing to accept the comforting lies. Don't let anyone take that from you."

The noise of the bar, the sad country song, the crack of pool balls—it all faded away. There was only the small, amber-lit world of their booth. There was only Liam, seeing her not as a problem to be solved, but as a person who had correctly identified the problem with the universe itself.

She felt deeply, thrillingly understood.

"I was so close to believing him," she confessed. "The professor. He was so... kind."

"Kindness is the prettiest cage," Liam said, his thumb stroking the back of her hand. "He's kind because his worldview has never been truly threatened. He can afford to be gentle. He's never had to fight for his own intellectual survival."

The space between them seemed to shrink, charged with an intensity that was more than just philosophical agreement. His gaze dropped to her mouth, then back to her eyes. She felt a familiar flutter in her chest, a feeling she'd thought was dead and buried. Attraction. Or at least, the desperate, grateful version of it.

He leaned closer, the scent of him—beer and cologne and the cold night air clinging to his jacket—filling her senses. "You don't need to be fixed," he murmured. "You just need to be heard."

When he kissed her, it was nothing like she expected. It wasn't a gentle exploration; it was a confirmation. A statement of fact. His lips were firm, demanding, and she met his pressure with her own. It tasted of beer and bitterness and the exhilarating relief of no longer being alone in her own head. It was a seal on a pact, an amen to a sermon she could finally believe in.

She wrapped her arms around his neck, pulling him closer, needing the solid, physical reality of him to anchor her. His hands tangled in her hair, his fingers pressing against her scalp, and the kiss deepened, becoming something hungry and desperate on both sides. This was real. This was a feeling she could trust. Not the abstract promise of a heavenly father or the hollow comfort of a prayer, but the undeniable presence of another person who saw the world in the same stark, unforgiving light.

It felt more grounding than any hymn ever had. More real than any sermon. It was a prayer answered with a warm body instead of a hollow silence.

And for the first time in a long time, Brianna felt like she might actually be saved.

She pulled back, breathless, her pulse hammering a wild rhythm against her throat. The low-wattage light of the bar seemed to have focused into a single, intense spotlight on their booth. She looked at Liam, truly looked at him, and saw none of the pity or gentle concern that had become the currency of her interactions. His eyes were dark with an intensity that bordered on triumph, his lips slightly swollen from their kiss. He wasn't looking at a grieving girl. He was looking at a convert.

"See?" he said, his voice a low, rough murmur. "Not so complicated. Just truth."

His thumb was still stroking the back of her hand, a slow, possessive rhythm that seemed to be mapping her bones. The gesture was grounding, a physical anchor in the swirling chaos of her thoughts. The world Dr. Finch had cracked open—a messy, complicated place of grief and love and angry prayers—snapped shut. Liam's world was a clean, stark binary: truth or lies, clarity or faith, us or them. It was a relief to know which side she was on.

"It feels..." she started, then trailed off, unsure how to describe the massive, internal shift that had just occurred.

"Like breathing after being held underwater for too long?" he supplied.

She nodded, a wave of gratitude so intense it almost felt like love washing over her. "Exactly."

He smiled, that slow, knowing smile that made her feel like he had excavated the deepest parts of her mind and found them familiar territory. He flagged down the bartender for another pitcher, the gesture easy and proprietary, as if they had been doing this for years.

"My mom used to love places like this," Brianna found herself saying, the memory bubbling up unbidden in the new intimacy between them. "Not dive bars, exactly, but diners with cracked vinyl and bad coffee. She said they were more honest than fancy restaurants. She said you could always tell the truth about a place by the state of its ketchup bottles."

It was a small, perfect memory, a shard of the woman her mother had been. She offered it to him like a gift.

Liam listened, but his eyes had a distant, analytical gleam. "That's a perfect example of the narrative instinct," he said, as if she'd just presented a piece of evidence for his thesis. "Humans are desperate to impose meaning on random data. Sticky ketchup bottles don't mean a place is honest. They mean the staff is underpaid and overworked. But it's a nicer story to believe they're a sign of authenticity, right? It makes the world feel less random. Less... cruel."

A tiny, cold flicker of disappointment went through her. He hadn't heard the love in the story. He hadn't seen her mother's face, her easy laugh. He'd only seen a data point, another example to support his all-encompassing theory. But the disappointment was immediately swamped by the force of his logic. He was right, of course. It was a childish, sentimental thought. Liam was teaching her to see the world without the soft-focus filter of sentimentality. It was a valuable lesson. A necessary one.

"You're right," she said, her voice a little quieter. "It's just a story."

"They're all just stories," he said, his hand finding hers again. "And we get to write our own. One that starts tonight."

They stayed until last call, the second pitcher of beer disappearing between them as they systematically dismantled the world she had grown up in. Every hymn was a form of mass hypnosis, every sermon a tool of crowd control, every potluck a performance of community that masked deep loneliness. It was a ruthless, exhilarating deconstruction. With every belief she surrendered, she felt lighter, freer, more completely herself. Or at least, more completely this new person she was becoming with his help.

When they finally stumbled out of The Alibi, the night air was shockingly cold and clean. The street was empty, the town asleep. Above them, a gash of stars was visible in the inky blackness, clear and indifferent.

Liam stopped under a streetlight, turning to face her. "No more looking for signs in the stars," he said, his voice soft but certain. "No more asking them for answers. We just get to look at them. And that's enough."

He was giving her the universe back, stripped of all the weighty expectations she'd placed on it. It wasn't a loving creation or a cruel joke. It just... was. And so was she.

He leaned in and kissed her again, a slow, sealing kind of kiss. It wasn't hungry and desperate like the one in the bar. It was a promise. A benediction. The final, quiet amen of the Gospel of Nothing.

As he walked her back toward the glowing lights of campus, his arm slung comfortably around her shoulders, Brianna felt a sense of peace settle over her for the first time in months. She had an answer. She had a framework. She had a person who understood. The path forward was no longer a terrifying, empty space. It was a road they would walk together, guided by the cold, clear, and beautiful light of their own disbelief.

The world, for a few weeks, became blessedly small. It was the size of their corner booth at The Alibi, the cramped space of Liam's dorm room that always smelled like unwashed laundry and old books, the two feet of pavement between them as they walked across campus, a unified front against the relentless optimism of college life. Liam's disbelief was a fortress, and Brianna lived inside its walls, grateful for the shelter.

Their life settled into a rhythm, a catechism of rebellion. Mondays and Wednesdays were for coffee and deconstruction, dismantling everything from the social contract to the concept of altruism. Tuesdays and Thursdays were for classes she attended with a new, critical detachment, seeing the hidden agendas and power structures beneath every lecture. Dr. Finch's class was the worst. She sat in the back, her laptop a literal and figurative shield, interpreting his every thoughtful question as a subtle manipulation, every kind smile as the condescending pat of the gentle shepherd. She saw him exactly as Liam had described him, and the clarity was a relief, absolving her of the confusing warmth she'd felt in his office.

And the weekends—the weekends were for noise.

Friday was the party at the lacrosse house, a crush of bodies moving under strobing lights, the bass a physical presence in her bones. She and Liam stood in a corner, providing a running, cynical commentary on the mating rituals of their peers. "See that guy?" Liam would murmur in her ear, his breath warm against her skin. "He's performing confidence to mask a deep-seated fear of mediocrity." Brianna would laugh, a sharp, bright sound that felt practiced. She drank whatever was handed to her, letting the alcohol build a pleasant haze between her and the world. The chaos that had once felt liberating now just felt... loud. A necessary anesthetic.

Saturday was the party at the off-campus apartment with the leaky ceiling, where the air was thick with the sweet, cloying smell of weed. She found herself in a conversation with a girl who was crying about a political science midterm. "It's all just so meaningless, you know?" the girl slurred, mascara tracking down her cheeks. Instead of feeling empathy, Brianna heard Liam's voice in her head, analyzing the girl's performative despair. She offered a few noncommittal platitudes and escaped back to Liam's side, feeling a flicker of something cold and ugly in her chest. She was becoming a very good student of his gospel.

The routine was a shield. When her father called on Sunday afternoon, his voice small and distant over the phone, she could answer from the cocoon of Liam's bed, his arm thrown possessively over her waist. "Just checking in, kiddo," her dad would say. "How are classes?" "Fine, Dad. Busy." "Are you... you know... meeting people? Making friends?" "I have a boyfriend," she'd say, and the statement was a shield in itself. *I am not alone. You don't need to worry. Stop asking.* "Oh. That's... that's great, Bree." The hesitation in his voice was palpable, the ghost of the name she no longer answered to hanging between them. Then, the question he always asked, the one that made her stomach clench: "Have you thought about finding a church? Just for the community?" "Dad, we've talked about this. That's not who I am anymore." Liam's logic would rise up, a ready defense. *Religion is a social construct. Community based on shared delusion is not community.* "I have to go. I have a lot of studying to do." She would hang up and ignore the wave of guilt that followed, turning instead to kiss Liam, letting his certainty drown out the quiet, lonely voice of her father.

Maya became a ghost in their room, a peripheral figure of quiet kindness Brianna learned to navigate around. One night, after a particularly draining party, Brianna stumbled in to find a cup of chamomile tea steaming on her desk and a note: *Tough night? Thinking of you.* The next morning, the tea was still there, cold and untouched. She poured it down the sink when Maya was in the shower, the act feeling both necessary and cruel. She could not afford to accept a kindness that came with no intellectual framework. It was a Trojan horse, and she had been warned.

The initial, exhilarating high of her new life began to flatten into a low-grade, persistent exhaustion. The parties blurred together, a repetitive cycle of sticky floors, shouting over music, and waking up with a headache and the taste of regret in her mouth. The intellectual sparring with Liam, which had once felt like a lifeline, started to feel like a performance. She found herself recycling his opinions, his phrases, his carefully constructed cynicism, until she wasn't sure where his thoughts ended and hers began.

One afternoon, studying in the library, she felt a sudden, sharp pang of longing for her mother so intense it stole her breath. It was a physical ache, a hollowing out in her chest. She immediately texted Liam: *The existential dread is hitting hard today.*

His reply came a minute later: *Anxiety is the dizziness of freedom. -Kierkegaard. It's a good sign. It means you're awake.*

The text should have been comforting. It was the language they spoke. But for a split second, all she wanted was for someone to say, *I'm so sorry. That must hurt so much.*

The thought was a betrayal, and she pushed it away, focusing on the Danish philosopher's words until her own ache felt like an intellectual concept instead of a wound.

The unraveling began, as it often does, in a quiet moment late on a Tuesday night. She and Liam had been at his place, watching a bleak French film about the futility of love. He had paused it every few minutes to deconstruct the director's nihilistic intentions. It wasn't a date; it was a lecture. When she finally got back to her room, the exhaustion was bone-deep. Maya was already asleep, her breathing a soft, steady rhythm in the quiet room.

Brianna went into their shared bathroom to wash her face, splashing cold water against her skin, trying to rinse away the sticky film of the party scene and the weight of a philosophy that was starting to feel heavier than the faith she'd abandoned. She looked up, catching her own eye in the mirror, and for the first time in weeks, she didn't immediately look away.

The girl staring back at her was a stranger.

Her face was pale and thin, the shadows under her eyes like bruises. Her hair was lank and unwashed. But it was her expression that was the most alien. The open, sunny face she remembered from photos with her mom was gone, replaced by something guarded and brittle. Her mouth was set in a tight, unimpressed line that was a perfect imitation of Liam's. Her eyes, which used to be her best feature, looked... empty. Stripped of all their light.

This was the face of freedom. This was the philosopher-warrior who had successfully shed the comforting lies of her past. She was awake. She was honest. She was intellectually rigorous.

And she had never, in her entire life, looked so profoundly and utterly alone.

The armor she and Liam had so carefully constructed—the cynicism, the anger, the Gospel of Nothing—suddenly felt less like a fortress and more like a cage. A very small, very cold cage, built for one. The thought was not a shout but a whisper, rising up from some deep, buried part of her she'd thought was long dead.

This isn't freedom, the voice whispered. *This is just a different kind of running.*

She leaned against the sink, her hands gripping the cool porcelain, and stared at the stranger in the mirror until her own reflection blurred, and all she could see was the ghost of the girl she used to be, asking her what in God's name she had done.

A shudder wracked her body, a violent, involuntary tremor that started in her gut and radiated out to her fingertips. She backed away from the mirror as if the reflection might reach out and grab her, her bare feet silent on the cold linoleum. Back in the dorm room, the darkness was a relief, a shroud for the stranger she'd just met. Maya's soft breathing was a steady, rhythmic anchor in the silence, a sound of life in a room that suddenly felt like a tomb.

Brianna slid into her bed, pulling the thin gray comforter up to her chin, but the cold wasn't on her skin. It was inside her, a deep, cellular chill that no blanket could warm. She closed her eyes, but the image from the mirror was seared onto the back of her eyelids: the hollow eyes, the tight mouth, the brittle emptiness. *This is just a different kind of running.* The whisper was louder now, insistent. She was running from the grief, yes, but she was also running from the girl who knew how to grieve—the one who would have cried, who would have prayed, who would have reached out. This new version, this philosopher-warrior, didn't know how to do any of those things. She only knew how to analyze, to deconstruct, to burn.

Sleep was a distant country she couldn't reach. Every time she drifted close, a memory would flash, sharp as a shard of glass. Her mother's hand on her forehead, checking for a fever. Her mother's laugh, rich and full, at one of her father's bad jokes. Her mother, sitting on the edge of her bed, the night before Brianna left for a week-long mission trip to Mexico, her face etched with a familiar mixture of pride and worry.

The memory bloomed, sudden and complete. Brianna had been sixteen, terrified of the trip, of sleeping on a church floor and speaking broken Spanish and failing to be the good, faithful servant everyone expected her to be.

"I can't do this," she'd whispered into the darkness of her bedroom, the confession feeling like a monumental failure. "I'm not... good enough. I'm scared."

Her mother hadn't offered platitudes. She hadn't quoted a Bible verse about courage. She'd just been quiet for a long moment, her hand finding Brianna's under the covers. Her skin was warm, her grip sure.

"Oh, honey," Sarah had said, her voice a soft, steady murmur. "Faith isn't about not being scared. That's not faith, that's just... being lucky." She squeezed Brianna's hand. "Faith is about being terrified and going anyway. It's about asking all your hard, angry questions in the middle of the night and trusting that Someone is still listening, even if you don't get an answer. You can be scared and still be held, Bree. They're not mutually exclusive."

The memory was so vivid, so present, that Brianna could almost feel the phantom pressure of her mother's hand around her own. *You can be scared and still be held.* The words were a direct contradiction to everything Liam preached. In his world, fear was a weakness to be analyzed away, a symptom of a belief in comforting lies. But her mother had treated fear as a given, a part of the human landscape, something to be carried, not conquered.

A wave of nausea, thick and sour, rose in her throat. She pushed off the bed, the room tilting slightly, and stumbled into the cold, sterile light of the bathroom. She leaned over the sink, bracing herself, and when she finally lifted her head, she met the eyes of a stranger in the mirror.

The woman staring back was a hollowed-out version of herself, a cruel caricature drawn by grief and cynicism. The light in her eyes, once a vibrant blue, had been snuffed out, leaving behind a flat, guarded emptiness. Her skin, usually flushed with life, was now a pallid, almost translucent gray, stretched taut over cheekbones that seemed too sharp for her face. A web of fine lines had gathered at the corners of her mouth—not from smiling, but from the constant effort of holding her features in a mask of detached indifference. Even her hair, once a wild cascade of copper, hung limp and lifeless.

A gasp, ragged and sharp, tore from her lips. Where was the girl who argued with joyful abandon? The woman who cried at sappy commercials and believed in the ridiculous, beautiful magic of a first snowfall? This creature in the glass hadn't believed in anything for years. Liam had promised her freedom—freedom from sentiment, from messy attach-ments, from the pain of caring too much. He had sold her a gospel of enlightened emptiness.

And here was the result. Not freedom, but a cage of her own making, its bars forged from his detached logic. She had analyzed away every part of herself that mattered, sanded down every soft edge until nothing remained but this hard, brittle shell. He had made her nothing.

A single, hot tear escaped, not tracing a gentle path but cutting a sharp, burning track down her temple. It was followed by another, then another, the salt stinging her chapped skin. She didn't turn into a pillow. She faced the stranger in the mirror, her body shaking with the first honest, ragged sobs she had allowed herself in months, mourning the woman she had executed in the name of being free.

Anger and intellectual arguments crashed over her, a merciless, cleansing wave. She wasn't just crying for her mother. She was crying for the girl who had believed she could be held, for the simple, profound comfort of that belief, a comfort she had willfully, systematically destroyed.

She didn't know how long she laid there, suffocating her sobs in her pillow, when a soft sound broke the rhythm of the room. The gentle creak of a mattress. A rustle of blankets.

Brianna froze, her breath catching in her throat. She squeezed her eyes shut, pretending to be asleep, her body rigid with the effort of stillness. She heard the soft pad of feet on the floor, then the click of a desk lamp, casting a warm, indirect glow. A drawer opened and closed. Water ran in the small sink in the corner. The clink of a ceramic mug.

She waited for the inevitable question. *Are you okay?* The question that would force her to lie or fall apart completely. She braced for it, her defenses rising automatically.

But the question never came.

Instead, she felt a slight dip in her mattress as a weight was placed on her nightstand. The footsteps retreated. The desk lamp clicked off. The mattress creaked again as Maya got back into bed. Then, only the sound of breathing in the dark.

After a long moment, Brianna slowly, carefully, turned her head. Sitting on her nightstand, illuminated by the faint moonlight from the window, was a steaming mug. From it rose the gentle, floral scent of chamomile tea.

No note. No whispered words of comfort. Just a cup of tea, left in the darkness. An offering that demanded nothing in return. Not thanks, not a conversation, not even acknowledgement. It was a simple, silent presence. A light left on in the dark.

The unconditional kindness of it bypassed every one of her carefully constructed defenses. Liam would have had a theory for this—the tyranny of care, an attempt to fix her, to ease Maya's own discomfort. But it didn't feel like tyranny. It felt like a hand, offered in the dark. A quiet testament that she was not as alone as she had made herself.

She didn't drink the tea. She couldn't. To accept the comfort would be to admit how desperately she needed it. But she didn't pour it out, either. She just lay there, on her side, watching the steam rise from the mug in the pale light, a silent, fragrant prayer in the space between their beds. It was a language she had almost forgotten how to speak, a gospel far older and quieter than Liam's. And for the first time in a long, long time, she didn't try to argue with it. She just let it be.

Chapter Seven

The Uncomfortable Truth

The world returned in muted gray. Brianna's eyelids peeled open, gritty and swollen. She woke not to an alarm, but to the quiet scratch of a pen on paper and the bitter, watery scent of long-stale chamomile. A distinct, physical ache radiated from the center of her chest, the ghost of a sob lodged deep in her throat. Her head throbbed with a dull, cottony pressure, the hangover of a grief finally uncorked. The cold ceramic of the mug on her nightstand was an artifact from another lifetime—last night—a silent testament to Maya's vigil through the long, dark hours. Every part of her felt tenderized, bruised from the inside out. She was fragile, like a photograph left out in the sun, her colors faded, her felt tenderized, bruised from the inside out.

Maya looked up, saw she was awake, and slipped her headphones off. Her expression was open, her eyes clear of last night's pity or concern. "Hey," she said, her voice a normal morning-raspy whisper. "There's one banana left. It's got a few brown spots, but I think it's still salvageable. All yours if you want it."

The sheer, unadulterated normalcy of the offer was a physical shock. No mention of the crying. No reference to the tea. Just a bruised banana, offered without agenda. It was a kindness so simple it had no room for subtext, no angle for deconstruction. It was just... nice.

"Oh," Brianna said. Her voice was a croak. "Thanks." The word felt rusty in her throat, an antique she hadn't used in months.

Maya just smiled, put her headphones back on, and returned to her highlighting.

Brianna swung her legs out of bed, her bare feet hitting the cold floor. She picked up the cold mug from her nightstand and walked to their small sink. As she poured the tea down the drain, the act felt different from the day before. It wasn't a defiant rejection. It was a quiet, necessary erasing of the evidence, because she didn't yet know what to do with the uncomfortable truth of it: that a simple, unanalyzed act of kindness had pierced her armor more effectively than any argument.

Her phone buzzed, a jarring, electronic summons back to the world she'd chosen. It was Liam.

The great beast of Academia awakens. Need to mainline some caffeine and righteous indignation before my 10 a.m. seminar on Postmodern Ethics. The Grind in 15?

The words, which yesterday would have felt like a secret handshake, a confirmation of their shared superiority, now read like a script. A set of lines she was expected to learn. The righteous indignation felt exhausting before it even began. But the alternative—sitting alone with this fragile, unfamiliar feeling of vulnerability—was unthinkable. She needed the noise. She needed the armor.

On my way, she typed back, the lie of her own enthusiasm a small, necessary betrayal of the girl who had cried in the dark.

The Grind was a different church, and Liam was its high priest. He was already holding court in a booth by the window, a half-empty mug of black coffee in his hand as he explained to another philosophy major why the concept of "safe spaces" was an intellectual oxymoron. He saw Brianna and his face lit up, not with warmth, but with the satisfaction of a general seeing his best soldier arrive for duty.

"Brianna," he said, sliding over to make room. "Just in time. We were dissecting the university's latest email on 'inclusive language.' A master-class in performative wokeness."

She slid onto the bench, the familiar scent of burnt coffee and Liam's cologne a Pavlovian trigger. This was her place. This was her catechism. She just had to remember the words.

"It's all about protecting the brand," she recited,

"...and you see it everywhere," he was saying, his voice gaining momentum. "This tyranny of forced optimism. People who think they can solve deep, existential pain with a motivational quote or some act of unsolicited kindness." He glanced at her, a sharp, knowing look. "Like those people who leave a cup of tea on your desk when you're having a bad night, thinking their herbal remedy is a match for the howling void of a meaningless universe."

The words hit the air with the force of a thrown rock. He couldn't have known. It was a coincidence, a lucky shot. But his eyes were on her, probing, testing. He was speaking their shared language, reminding her of their core tenets. He was calling her back to the faith.

The other student laughed. "The worst," he agreed. "My roommate tried to get me to do 'gratitude journaling.' As if listing three things I'm grateful for is going to fix late-stage capitalism."

They both looked at Brianna, waiting for her to join in, to add her own cynical amen. The silence stretched. The old Brianna, the one from forty-eight hours ago, would have had a sharp, cutting remark ready. She would have performed her part flawlessly.

But the girl who had watched the steam rise from a cup of tea in the moonlight couldn't find her voice. All she could think of was the quiet click of Maya's lamp, the gentle pad of her feet on the floor. The simple, human act of showing up in the dark.

"Maybe," Brianna said, her voice barely a whisper, "she was just trying to be nice."

The words dropped into the conversation like a stone in a silent pond. The other student stared at her, confused. But Liam's expression shifted instantly, the amused superiority draining away, replaced by a cold, sharp-edged watchfulness. He had heard the heresy.

"'Nice' is the word people use when they don't have the courage to be honest," he said, his voice flat. "It's a social lubricant for people who are terrified of friction."

"Or maybe," she said, looking directly at him, a strange, terrifying courage rising in her, "it's just... kindness. Maybe it doesn't have to mean anything else."

Liam's jaw tightened. He leaned in, his voice dropping so the other student couldn't hear. "What's going on with you? You're talking like one of *them*. Don't tell me you're falling for the comforting lies again, Brianna. I thought you were stronger than that."

The accusation in his voice—*stronger than that*—should have stung. Instead, it illuminated the central flaw in his entire gospel. To him, strength was the absence of softness. It was a refusal of comfort, a rejection of hope. It was a hardness, a brittleness. She thought of the stranger in the mirror, her face a mask of that same brittle strength. She thought of Maya, who had faced her own profound loss and had come out the other side not hard, but relentlessly, defiantly kind. And she suddenly, terrifyingly, wasn't sure which one was stronger.

"I'm just tired, Liam," she said, the excuse a thin shield for a much more complicated truth.

"Tired of what? Thinking for yourself?" The question was a scalpel, intended to cut her away from this sudden, dangerous sentimentality. But for the first time, his intellectual bullying felt clumsy, desperate. She saw him not as a brilliant philosopher, but as a scared boy, frantically shoring up the walls of his own fortress. His dogma was just as rigid, just as demanding, as the one he'd fled.

She didn't argue. She didn't try to explain the cup of tea or the memory of her mother's hand or the stranger in the mirror. He had no language for those things. His worldview had no room for them.

She stood up, her chair scraping against the concrete floor. "I have to go," she said. "I forgot I have to prep for a quiz."

Liam stared up at her, his face a mixture of anger and disbelief. He had lost control of the narrative, and he didn't know what to do. "Brianna," he said, his voice a low command. "Don't."

Don't what? Don't leave? Don't think this way? Don't break the rules of our shared religion?

She just looked at him, and in that moment, she felt a profound, aching pity. For him. For the small, airless world he had built for himself, a world where every kindness was a manipulation and every flicker of hope was a lie. It was a safe world, in its own way. Nothing could ever hurt you if you'd already decided it was all meaningless. But nothing could ever reach you, either.

"I'll text you later," she said, a lie they both recognized.

She walked out of The Grind, leaving him in the middle of his own sermon. The bright autumn air felt shockingly clean after the stale atmosphere of the coffee shop. She didn't feel triumphant. She didn't feel free. She felt completely and utterly adrift.

The Gospel of Nothing had been a simple, elegant answer to the chaos of her grief. But what if the answer was wrong? The uncomfortable truth settled into her bones, cold and heavy as stone: she had fled the ruins of one faith only to build a new church on even shakier ground. And now, for the first time, she was standing in the wreckage of them both, with no idea where to even begin to look for shelter.

"Some shelters aren't meant to be homes," he said, his voice a quiet counterpoint to the rustling leaves. "Think of that faith you grew up in. For you, it was a cathedral, wasn't it? Vast and beautiful. But you began to see the cracks in the foundation, the rot in the beams. You realized the whole magnificent structure was unsafe.

So you began the terrifying work of demolition. But you can't tear down a building like that without getting hurt by the falling stone. So you built scaffolding—a stark, cold framework of cynicism to protect yourself. It was necessary. It let you stand at a safe distance and see the flaws for what they were. It shielded you while you did the hard, painful work of tearing down what you once loved. The problem, Brianna, is that we can get so used to the scaffolding—its rigid lines, its bitter safety—that we forget it isn't a house. It's a cage open to the wind. Nothing can grow there. Its purpose is to be temporary. It's meant to be taken down, piece by piece, once the ground is clear, so you can finally stand on solid earth and begin to build something new. Something honest. Something that is truly yours."

Panic seized her. Her first, animal instinct was to turn and flee, to disappear back into the anonymous flow of student life. It was what she had done last time, fleeing the quiet truth of his office for the loud lies of The Alibi. But her legs wouldn't obey. The exhaustion was too deep. The lies had run out of fuel. There was nowhere left to run.

She walked, putting one foot in front of the other because it was the only instruction her body could remember how to follow. The campus, which moments ago had been a familiar landscape, now felt alien and hostile. The cheerful shouts of a frisbee game on the quad sounded like a language from another planet. The bright, crisp autumn air felt too thin to breathe. Every smiling face that passed was a judgment, every burst of easy laughter an accusation. She had no allegiance, no creed, no corner of this world that wasn't reading. He was just sitting, a thermos of what she assumed was coffee beside him, watching the wind send a cascade of rust-colored leaves skittering across the flagstones. He looked up as she approached, his perceptive gaze taking in her wild, hunted expression.

So she just stopped, ten feet from his bench, her arms wrapped around herself as if to hold her splintering pieces together.

He didn't smile the gentle, paternal smile she dreaded. He didn't look concerned or alarmed. He simply looked at her, his expression one of quiet, patient recognition, as if he had been expecting a lost traveler to appear on this path all along.

"It's a fine day for getting lost," he said, his voice a low rumble that didn't startle the air.

The simple, observational truth of it—not a question, but a statement of fact—cracked something open in her chest.

"I think," she said, the words catching in her throat, raw and broken, "I think I just burned down my only shelter."

He considered this for a moment, his eyes on the scattering leaves. "Some shelters aren't meant to last," he said finally. "Some are just scaffolding. We build them to protect ourselves while we're doing the hard work of tearing down an even older, more dangerous building. The problem is, we can get so used to the scaffolding that we forget it was never meant to be a home."

He patted the empty space on the bench beside him. It was an invitation, not a command. Hesitantly, like an animal approaching a fire, she moved forward and sat, perching on the very edge, ready to bolt.

They sat in silence for a long time, the only sound the rustle of the leaves and the distant chime of the campus clock tower. He didn't push. He didn't ask for details. He just shared the silence, letting it be a space she could occupy without having to perform or defend herself.

"After my son died," he said, his gaze still fixed on the middle distance, "I tried to build a fortress of my own. Out of books. Logic. The cold, hard fact of biological determinism. It was very sturdy. Impenetrable." He took a slow sip from his thermos. "And it was a terribly cold place to live. It kept the grief out, for a time. But it kept everything else out, too. Love. Memory. The impossible, illogical, and deeply human hope that you might one day feel the sun on your face and not find it an insult."

Brianna stared at her hands, twisted together in her lap. He was speaking a language she was only just beginning to understand. The language of the hollowed-out.

"What did you do?" she asked, her voice small.

"Nothing, for a very long time," he said. "I just stayed in my cold, logical fortress and froze. Until one day, my wife—who had been patiently waiting outside the walls for years—simply came and sat by the gate. She didn't demand I come out. She didn't try to tear it down. She just brought a blanket and a thermos of her own, and she sat. And in her sitting, she reminded me that I wasn't just a mind that could be shielded by arguments. I was a man who was cold. And there was warmth, just on the other side of the wall, if I was ever brave enough to want it again."

He turned to look at her then, and his eyes were filled not with pity, but with a profound and steady empathy. "Being without a shelter is a terrifying thing, Brianna. But it is also the only state in which you can ever hope to build a true home. One with windows. And a door that opens from the inside."

The words didn't fix anything. They didn't offer a solution or a path forward. They simply named the place where she was: a desolate, terrifying, and strangely sacred patch of open ground. He had given her permission to be shelterless. He had validated the terror of it, while gently suggesting that it might not be an end, but a beginning.

A single tear traced a path through the dust on her cheek. She didn't bother to wipe it away.

"I don't know how," she whispered. "I don't know how to build anything."

"No one ever does, at first," Dr. Finch said, his voice impossibly kind. "You just find one true thing to build on. A memory. A kindness. A cup of tea left on a nightstand. And you start there."

The quiet, specific mention of the tea was a gentle shock. He couldn't know. But somehow, he did. He saw it all.

She finally looked up, meeting his gaze, and for the first time, she didn't feel seen in a way that made her want to hide. She felt seen in a way that made her feel real. The hollow stranger in the mirror began to recede, replaced by a girl who was heartbroken and lost and exhausted, but who was, undeniably, still there.

She stayed on that bench long after Dr. Finch had wished her a good afternoon and rumbled his way back into the brick building. She watched the light change, the shadows of the old oak tree stretching long across the lawn. The frantic panic in her chest had subsided, replaced by a vast, quiet, and terrifying stillness.

She was adrift. She was shelterless. She was standing on the empty ground where two inadequate churches had fallen.

And for the first time, she didn't immediately start looking for new materials to build another wall. She just sat, breathing the cold, clear, honest air, and waited to see what the truth felt like.

The world, when she finally re-entered it, had not changed. The clock tower still chimed the hour, students still hurried along the paths with backpacks slung over their shoulders, and the sky was still a vast, indifferent blue. But Brianna had changed. She walked back to Hawthorne Hall as if returning to a foreign country whose language she had forgotten. The key in the lock, the squeak of the hinges, the familiar geography of her room—it all felt alien, a set for a play whose lines she no longer knew.

She stood in the middle of the room, a ghost in her own life. The angry band poster on her wall looked childish now, a petulant scrawl. Her grey comforter, once a statement of defiant numbness, just looked sad. The silence was absolute, a high, ringing frequency in her ears now that the constant, frantic noise of her own internal arguments had ceased. The fortress was gone, the scaffolding had been kicked away, and she was left standing in a field of rubble, shivering in the sudden, shocking exposure.

When Maya came in an hour later, loaded down with books, Brianna was still sitting on the edge of her bed, staring at the dust motes dancing in the slice of light from the window. She had not moved. She had not thought. She had simply been.

Maya stopped just inside the door, her usual bright energy softening as she took in the scene. She didn't ask what was wrong. She didn't offer a chipper greeting. She simply absorbed the quiet, heavy atmosphere of the room and adjusted herself to it. It was an act of profound, unconscious empathy, and it was the second time in as many days that Maya's quiet intuition had disarmed her completely.

"Long day?" Maya asked, her voice soft. She dropped her heavy bag by her desk with a muffled thud.

Brianna nodded, the movement feeling slow and disconnected. "Something like that."

"I was going to grab a salad from the dining hall," Maya said, pulling her hair out of its messy bun and shaking her curls free. "Probably something with a questionable amount of ranch dressing. Want to come?"

The invitation was so simple, so mundane. It was a lifeline disguised as a dinner plan. The Brianna of last week would have had an excuse ready—studying, a headache, plans with Liam. The Brianna of this moment, however, had nothing. No armor, no script, no fortress to hide in.

"Okay," she heard herself say. The word felt strange and new on her tongue.

In the dining hall, the familiar chaos felt different. The clatter of trays, the scrape of chairs, the roar of a hundred simultaneous conversations—it was no longer a welcome cacophony to drown in. It was just noise. For the first time, Brianna felt separate from it, an observer rather than a participant in the frantic performance of college life.

They found a small table in a corner, away from the main flow of traffic. For a few minutes, they just sat in silence. Maya sighed dramatically. "It's times like this I wish I'd majored in something cool, like... I don't know, pirate history."

A small, rusty sound escaped Brianna's throat. It took her a second to identify it as a laugh. It was weak and hesitant, but it was real. "Is pirate history a major?"

"It should be," Maya said with a grin. "Way more interesting than the Krebs cycle, I guarantee you."

It was so... normal. A conversation about a boring class. A joke about pirates. There was no hidden agenda, no gentle prodding, no therapeutic subtext. It was just a roommate, being a roommate.

Her phone buzzed on the table beside her salad. It was Liam.

The phone in her hand felt less like a device and more like a talisman of his influence, cold and impossibly heavy. Her thumb trembled as it hovered over his name. The letters on the screen seemed to pulse with a faint light, a sigil representing the entire architecture of anxiety he had built inside her.

Where are you? I've been texting. Thought we were going to The Alibi.

Another buzz, a second later.

Don't let the old man get in your head. His kindness is a weapon. Remember?

She stared at the words. *His kindness is a weapon.* A few hours ago, that had been gospel. Now, sitting across from Maya, who had just offered her a joke about pirates and the quiet gift of her undemanding presence, Liam's words felt like a paranoid delusion. A desperate, frightened attempt to make the world small and ugly enough to control.

She felt a flicker of the old anger, but it wasn't directed at God or Dr. Finch. It was a flare of protective rage on behalf of a cup of tea. On behalf of a bruised banana. On behalf of all the small, simple kindnesses his philosophy had no room for.

With a strange sense of finality, she picked up the phone, held her thumb over Liam's name, and blocked his number. The action was quiet, simple, and more liberating than any party had ever been. She had not won an argument. She had simply walked off the battlefield.

She put the phone away, face down.

"Everything okay?" Maya asked, her gaze gentle.

"Yeah," Brianna said, and was surprised to find that for the first time in a long time, it wasn't a lie. "Everything's fine."

She turned her head on the pillow, her gaze drifting across the room to where Maya's fairy lights were on. Tonight, they weren't the cold, distant glitter of accusatory stars, each one a pinprick of judgment in her private sky. They had returned to being what they were: a string of tiny, earthbound suns. A humble constellation offering not cosmic truth, but human warmth, a quiet testament to the choice to be vulnerable in the face of the void.

For the first time, Brianna didn't flinch from their glow. The familiar urge to turn away, to retreat into the cynical armor she knew so well, simply dissolved. She just watched them burn, these small, brave affirmations against the vast and complicated dark, and felt something inside her declare a quiet, tentative truce. A thawing. She let their light fill her eyes, this fragile, man-made hope, and wondered. Wondered what it might feel like, one day, to build a life made not of walls, but of windows, and to finally trust the light to come pouring in.

That night, the silence in the dorm room was different again. It was no longer a ringing void or a space heavy with unspoken tension. It was just quiet. Brianna lay in her bed, the grey comforter pulled up to her chin, and listened to the sound of Maya turning the pages of her textbook.

She thought of Dr. Finch's words. *You just find one true thing to build on. A memory. A kindness... And you start there.*

She wasn't ready for the memories. They were still a landscape of ruins, too painful to excavate. But the kindness... the kindness was a single, solid stone in the palm of her hand. A cup of tea. A shared salad. A joke about pirates. It wasn't a fortress. It wasn't even a foundation. But it was something to hold onto in the dark.

Chapter Eight

The Quiet

The first thing Brianna noticed on Wednesday morning was the silence. It wasn't the peaceful quiet of an empty house or the studious hush of a library. It was an active, ringing silence, occupying the space where Liam's good-morning text should have been. Her phone lay dark on her nightstand, a blank slate, and the absence of his notification was a physical void. For weeks, his voice—via text, in person, in her own head—had been her morning coffee and her evening sedative. Now, there was just the hum of the mini-fridge and the soft scratch of Maya's highlighter on a textbook page.

She had spent the previous day in a fog, moving through her classes like a ghost, her mind a field of rubble she was too exhausted to excavate. She'd answered Maya's questions about her day with a few brief words , and Maya, with that unnerving intuition, had simply let her be. The quiet between them hadn't been a wall; it had been a space, held open.

"Morning," Maya said now, not looking up from her work. "I saved you the last of the decent coffee. The stuff they're brewing downstairs today smells like burnt sadness."

Brianna sat up, the gray comforter pooling around her. "Thanks." The word came out easier this time, less like a foreign object in her mouth. She poured a mug, the warmth seeping into her cold hands. She took a sip and leaned against the doorframe, watching her roommate. Maya's brow was furrowed in concentration, a stray curl falling across her forehead. Her side of the room, with its thriving plants and tacked-up photos of smiling friends, looked less like an accusation and more like a different country, one with a warmer climate.

"What are you working on?" Brianna asked, the question an awkward, unpracticed attempt at normalcy.

Maya looked up, surprised and pleased. "Abnormal Psych. Trying to figure out the difference between schizoid and schizotypal personality disorders. It's... a lot."

The old Brianna, Liam's Brianna, would have had a cynical comment ready. *The real disorder is thinking you can neatly categorize the chaos of the human mind.* The thought rose up out of habit, a ghost in her mental machine. But she swallowed it down. It tasted like ash.

"Sounds hard," she said instead.

"Tell me about it." Maya stretched, her arms reaching for the ceiling. "Sometimes I think the only thing separating 'normal' from 'abnormal' is how well you hide the weird." She grinned, and it was so open, so free of artifice, that Brianna had to look away.

That Friday, the silence grew teeth. The sun set, the campus came alive with the electric hum of weekend possibility, and a profound, terrifying loneliness descended on Brianna. For the past month, Friday night had meant Liam. It had meant a destination, a script, a purpose. Now, it was just a gaping hole in the week.

She could hear the sounds of girls getting ready in the rooms down the hall—the blast of a hairdryer, the tinny beat of a pre-game playlist, bursts of high-pitched laughter. She sat on her bed, scrolling through her phone with no real intention. Her feed was a curated stream of joy she couldn't access. Maya had gone out with some friends from her ministry group, leaving with a casual, "Have a good night! Text if you need anything!" that was both a kindness and a confirmation of Brianna's utter solitude.

An hour passed. Then another. The loneliness began to feel like a physical pressure, a tightening in her chest. The quiet of the room was too loud. She needed noise. She needed distraction. The old habits, the well-worn paths of her flight, called to her.

I can do it alone, she thought, the idea a small, desperate spark. *I don't need him to go to a party.*

The decision felt less like a choice and more like a surrender to momentum. She pulled on the familiar uniform—black jeans, band t-shirt, boots—but as she looked in the mirror, she saw what she'd seen the other night: a girl in a costume. Still, it was better than sitting here, drowning in the quiet.

The party was at a fraternity house she vaguely recognized, the one with the broken porch light. The same vibrating bass, the same smell of stale beer and desperation. But walking through the door alone was completely different. Without Liam as her anchor and interpreter, she was just... a girl at a party. No one knew her. No one spoke to her. She was invisible.

She got a cup of whatever was in the keg and found a spot against a wall, trying to look like she was waiting for someone. She watched the scenes she used to participate in. A couple was having a tearful, drunken argument by the fireplace. A group of guys were shouting over a game of beer pong, their laughter brittle and performative. A girl sat on the stairs, her face illuminated by her phone, looking just as lost as Brianna felt.

Before, Liam's running commentary would have made it all feel like an intellectual exercise, a sociological study. He would have pointed out the power dynamics, the mating rituals, the desperate need for validation. His cynicism was a shield that made it interesting instead of just sad.

Without the shield, it was just sad.

These weren't philosopher-warriors rejecting a broken system. They were just lonely kids, trying to numb whatever they were running from, just like her. The noise wasn't a triumphant rebellion; it was a desperate attempt to drown out the silence. The chaos wasn't freedom; it was just a mess.

She stayed for twenty-three minutes. She knew because she checked her phone obsessively. Then, placing her full, untouched cup on a cluttered end table, she slipped out the door. No one noticed.

The walk back to the dorm was quiet, the cold air a welcome shock to her system. The stars were out, clear and sharp in the black sky. Dr. Finch's words echoed in her memory. *It kept the grief out... but it kept everything else out, too.* Liam's fortress had kept her safe, but it had also kept her a prisoner. And she had been its only inhabitant.

Back in the empty room, the silence didn't feel like a void anymore. It felt like a clearing. A space to stand, however unsteady, on her own two feet. She sat on her bed, the sounds of the campus faint and distant through the closed window.

On impulse, she picked up her phone and scrolled to her father's contact. Her thumb hovered over the call button. The last few times they'd spoken, her voice had been a blade, sharpened by Liam's logic. She had cut him off, dismissed his concern, treated his grief as an inconvenience. A wave of shame, cold and sharp, washed over her.

She pressed the button before she could change her mind.

He picked up on the second ring, his voice wary. "Bree? Is everything okay?"

The sound of her old nickname, the one he clung to, made her throat tighten. "It's Brianna, Dad." The correction came out automatically, a reflex of her old armor. But she softened it. "And yeah. Everything's okay. I just... wanted to call."

There was a pause on the other end, filled with surprise and what sounded like relief. "Oh. Well, that's... that's nice, honey. How was your week?"

"It was okay. Classes are fine." The usual script. But this time, she tried for something more. "My lit professor is interesting. We're reading a lot of poetry."

"Poetry? Your mother loved poetry." The words were quiet, a memory shared carefully, as if it might break. "She used to read me Mary Oliver when I couldn't sleep. Said it was better than pills."

Brianna's chest ached. She remembered. The slim, worn volume of poems on her mother's nightstand. "Yeah. I remember."

Another silence, but this one felt different. Less like a chasm, more like a shared breath.

"How are... how are you, Dad?" she asked, the question feeling monumental.

He sighed, a long, weary sound that seemed to carry the weight of the whole year. "Getting by, I guess. The house is too quiet. I keep thinking I hear her coming down the stairs."

The confession was so simple, so vulnerable, it cracked clean through her. He wasn't the stoic, emotionally distant father she'd painted him as. He was just a man who was lost, same as her.

"I know," she whispered.

They didn't solve anything. They didn't have a breakthrough or a tearful reconciliation. They just talked for ten minutes about nothing and everything—about the leaky faucet he'd finally fixed, about a funny thing that had happened at his work, about the weather. It was the most normal conversation they'd had in months.

"Well," he said finally, "I should let you go. Probably got studying to do."

"Not really." The admission was a small act of trust. "I'm just hanging out."

"Okay." He sounded pleased. "Well, you take care of yourself, kiddo. I love you."

"I love you too, Dad," she said, and was surprised to find that the words didn't catch in her throat. They felt true.

When she hung up, the room was still quiet. But it wasn't a lonely quiet anymore. It was a peaceful one. The call hadn't fixed the gaping hole in her life, but it had built a thin, fragile bridge across a small piece of it. It was a start.

She was pulling back her covers when Maya came in, her cheeks flushed from the cold.

"Hey," Maya said, dropping her keys in a bowl on her desk. "Decided on a quiet night after all?"

"Yeah," Brianna said. "I think I'm done with parties for a while."

Maya just nodded, accepting the statement without question. She began her nightly routine—washing her face, brushing her teeth, changing into an old t-shirt. Brianna watched her, this girl she had held at arm's length for so long. This girl whose quiet, steady kindness had been a light she hadn't realized she was steering by.

As Maya climbed into bed, she glanced over at Brianna. "You know," she said casually, "if you're ever bored on a Sunday morning... we don't just do church stuff. A bunch of us just go for brunch at that diner downtown. The one with the questionable ranch dressing."

It wasn't an invitation to church. It wasn't a plea to find her faith again. It was just an offer of pancakes. A place to be, on a day that was hard, with people who might not have all the answers, but who knew how to show up.

Brianna thought of the cold fortress she had lived in for so long. Then she thought of a home with windows.

"Maybe," she said, and the word held more possibility than anything she'd said in months. "I'll think about it."

She turned off her light and lay in the dark, listening to the quiet rhythm of the room. She was shelterless. She was standing on cleared ground. And for the first time, the thought of building something new didn't feel terrifying. It felt, strangely, like hope.

The quiet settled in her bones, a fine silt layering over the raw nerve endings of the past few weeks. On Saturday, Brianna woke up and for the first time, her immediate thought wasn't of Liam—not his absence, not his words, not the cage he'd built. The silence in her head was her own. It was a vast, empty landscape, and while it was terrifying, it was also hers to explore. She moved through the day with a strange, careful slowness, as if learning to walk again. She did her laundry. She bought a coffee that tasted only of coffee. She sat on a bench on the quad and watched a squirrel bury an acorn with frantic, single-minded determination, and felt a kinship with its small, urgent purpose.

She was trying to study in their room that afternoon, the pages of her history textbook blurring into meaningless blocks of text, when her gaze drifted to Maya's windowsill. A row of succulents, fat and green and stubbornly alive, soaked up the afternoon sun. One of them had sent up a thin, improbable stalk, a tiny pink flower blooming at its tip. It was a ridiculous, hopeful little flag waved in the face of everything.

It reminded her of her mother's garden. The way Sarah had treated the soil like a sacred text, her hands always plunged deep in the dark, rich earth. She'd called it her dirt therapy, her most honest form of prayer. Brianna closed her eyes, and the memory bloomed, sudden and complete.

It was a Tuesday in late July, oppressively hot, the air thick enough to drink. Her mother was in her favorite armchair in the sunroom, a faded quilt pulled up to her waist despite the heat. She had lost so much weight that the chair seemed to swallow her whole. Outside, her garden was in the full, chaotic riot of high summer, but weeds were beginning to creep in at the edges, a subtle, creeping neglect that mirrored the one happening inside her mother's body.

Brianna, seventeen and vibrating with a fury too big for her own skin, stood in the doorway, clutching a sheaf of papers from the oncologist's office. They were new printouts, new protocols, new statistics that all said the same thing in different, clinical ways: the first treatment hadn't worked.

"They want to try a different chemo," Brianna said, her voice flat and hard. "The one with the side effects we talked about." The one that would make her lose her hair for sure. The one that might not work either.

Her mother didn't look at the papers. She just kept her gaze fixed on the black-eyed Susans bobbing in the breeze. "Okay, honey."

That was it. Just, *Okay, honey*. The calm acceptance of it was a lit match to Brianna's carefully contained rage.

"Okay?" Brianna's voice cracked, rising. "That's it? Just 'okay'? Don't you want to fight? Don't you want to scream? How can you just sit there and talk about God's plan when this is happening? There is no plan! It's just random, stupid cells eating you alive while you quote Bible verses!"

The words were cruel, and she knew it. She wanted them to be. She wanted to crack the placid, infuriating peace on her mother's face, to make her feel even a fraction of the frantic, clawing terror that lived in Brianna's own chest.

Sarah turned her head slowly, her blue eyes, faded but still so clear, finding Brianna's. There was no hurt in them. Only a deep, bottomless sorrow. She didn't offer a platitude. She didn't defend God. She told the truth.

"Oh, honey, I'm terrified," she said, her voice a reedy whisper that was still the strongest thing Brianna had ever heard. "Every single minute. I wake up in the middle of the night and my heart is hammering so loud I think it's going to break right through my ribs. I'm so, so scared."

The confession disarmed Brianna completely. Her anger, with nothing to push against, collapsed inward, leaving only the aching grief it had been hiding. She sank to the floor, her shoulders slumping.

"Then how?" Brianna whispered. "How do you do it? How do you still... believe?"

Her mother was quiet for a long moment, watching a goldfinch land on the bird feeder. "I think," she said, choosing her words with the care of a gardener planting seeds, "that you and I have a different idea of what faith is. You think it's a feeling. A big, warm, certain feeling that everything is going to be okay." She smiled, a faint, tired curve of her lips. "I used to think that too. But that's not faith. That's just... being lucky."

She reached out a thin, papery hand, and Brianna crawled over and took it, her mother's skin cool and dry against her own.

"Faith, for me," Sarah continued, her gaze turning inward, "is about being terrified and showing up anyway. It's about asking all my hard, angry, screaming questions in the middle of the night and trusting that Someone is still listening, even if I don't get an answer I like. It's not about having the answers, Bree. It's about trusting you're not alone with the questions." She squeezed Brianna's hand, her grip surprisingly strong.

"You can be scared and still be held," she'd said, her eyes locking with her daughter's, willing her to understand. "They're not mutually exclusive."

Brianna opened her eyes. The dorm room was quiet, the afternoon light beginning to fade. The memory wasn't just a painful ghost this time. It landed differently. It was a key, clicking into a lock she hadn't known was there. Dr. Finch's words about anger being a cry of love. Maya's quiet, persistent kindness. Her father's lonely confession on the phone. They were all pieces of the same puzzle.

You can be scared and still be held.

She had thought her anger was a sign of her faith's death. But what if, as her mother and Dr. Finch had both suggested, it was proof that it was still alive, just in its most wounded and desperate form? She had been screaming her questions into the void, furious at the silence. She had never considered that the act of screaming itself was the faith.

She stood up and walked over to Maya's side of the room. She reached out and gently touched the velvety leaf of one of the succulents. It was sturdy, alive, full of a quiet, resilient life she didn't understand.

The weekend passed in that same quiet, contemplative state. She read for her classes. She took a long walk around the campus lake, watching the wind ripple the water. The silence in her phone felt less like an absence and more like an open space. A clearing.

On Saturday night, Maya was getting ready to go to a movie with a friend. As she was pulling on her boots, she paused.

"So, that brunch thing tomorrow," she said, her tone deliberately casual. "It's at ten. At the diner. No agenda. Just pancakes and people."

Brianna looked up from her book. Tomorrow was Sunday. The day God took her mother. The day she had decided He could have back. The thought of it still sent a familiar chill of dread through her.

But the memory of her mother's voice was a quiet counterpoint. *It's about being terrified and showing up anyway.*

Showing up to a party had been a flight from the quiet. Showing up to brunch... that felt like a step toward it. It wasn't a return to church. It wasn't a promise to start believing again. It was just pancakes. It was an experiment. A test of her mother's last, most important piece of advice.

Could she be scared—could she be angry and broken and utterly unsure of everything—and still allow herself to be held, even just for an hour, in the simple, uncomplicated community of a shared meal?

Maya was watching her, her expression open, expecting nothing.

"What time did you say?" Brianna asked.

Chapter Nine

The Seed of Hope

The memory ambushed her during Professor Martinez's American History lecture, triggered by something as simple as the way afternoon light slanted through the tall classroom windows—that particular golden quality of late October sun that made everything look like it was suspended in amber. One moment Brianna was dutifully taking notes about the Great Depression, and the next she was sixteen again, sitting cross-legged on her bedroom floor while her mother sorted through old photo albums, preparing for what they didn't yet know would be one of their last normal afternoons together.

It was a Saturday in early November, two years ago. The leaves outside Brianna's bedroom window were the same burnished gold as today's light, and her mother had declared it "Memory Day"—one of her spontaneous projects that usually involved reorganizing something while telling stories. This time it was the family photo albums, years of memories scattered across Brianna's comforter in neat piles organized by decade.

"Oh, look at this one," her mother had said, holding up a photo of five-year-old Brianna in a Halloween costume—an angel with crooked wings and a halo that kept sliding over one eye. "You insisted on being an angel three years in a row. Do you remember why?"

Brianna had rolled her eyes with the practiced exasperation of a teenager being subjected to childhood photos. "Because I thought angels were the most beautiful things in the world?"

"Because," her mother corrected gently, "you said angels were the ones who got to take care of people. You wanted to be the one taking care of everyone else."

The memory had that golden, soft-focus quality that distance lends to moments that seemed ordinary when they were happening. Her mother's voice, warm with affection and something else—pride, maybe, or recognition of something essential in her daughter's character that Brianna herself hadn't yet learned to see.

"I was worried about you sometimes," Sarah had continued, setting the photo aside and reaching for another stack. "You felt everything so deeply, even as a little girl. Happy or sad, you experienced it with your whole body. I used to watch you playing with your dolls, and you'd be so concerned about their feelings, making sure none of them felt left out."

"That's embarrassing, Mom."

"It's beautiful, honey. But I worried it would be hard for you when you got older. When you realized that you can't fix everyone's pain, that caring deeply sometimes means getting hurt deeply."

Brianna had been only half-listening then, more interested in the photos themselves than her mother's philosophical observations about her childhood personality. But something in her mother's tone—a weight, a deliberateness—had made her look up.

Sarah was staring out the window at the golden afternoon, her fingers absently tracing the edge of a photo she hadn't shown Brianna yet. There was something different about her expression, a distance that hadn't been there moments before.

"Mom? You okay?"

Her mother had turned back to her with that bright smile that Brianna now recognized as forced. "Of course, sweetheart. Just thinking." She held up the hidden photo—a picture of the two of them at Brianna's baptism, both glowing with pride and certainty. "I was remembering this day. How sure you were about everything. How clear your faith felt."

"It did feel clear then," Brianna admitted. "Everything seemed so... black and white. Good and bad, right and wrong, faithful and faithless."

"And now?"

Even at sixteen, Brianna had been starting to encounter questions that didn't have easy answers. Youth group discussions that felt too simple, prayers that seemed to echo in empty rooms, the growing awareness that terrible things happened to good people regardless of how much faith they had.

"Now it feels more complicated," she said.

Her mother had nodded, still looking at the baptism photo. "I want to tell you something, Bree. Something I probably should have told you before."

The seriousness in her voice made Brianna pay attention in a way she hadn't been moments before. She set down the photos she'd been sorting and faced her mother fully.

"Faith isn't supposed to stay simple," Sarah said quietly. "If it does, it's not really faith—it's just... childhood. Real faith, the kind that can carry you through the hardest parts of life, has to be big enough to hold questions. It has to be strong enough to survive doubt."

She pulled her knees up, wrapping her arms around them in a gesture that made her look younger, more vulnerable. "When I was your age, I thought faith meant having all the right answers. I thought doubt was the enemy, that good Christians were supposed to be certain about everything all the time."

"And now?"

"Now I think doubt might be faith's best friend. It's what keeps faith honest. It's what forces it to grow." Sarah looked directly at Brianna, her brown eyes intense with the need to communicate something important. "Honey, there are going to be times in your life when God feels absent. When prayers seem to bounce off the ceiling. When people you love suffer in ways that make no sense, and all the Sunday school answers feel like lies."

The prediction felt heavy with foreboding, though Brianna couldn't have known then how prophetic it would prove to be.

"What do I do when that happens?"

"You keep asking the hard questions. You refuse to accept easy answers that don't match what you're experiencing. And you remember that being angry at God is not the same thing as not believing in God. Sometimes anger is the most honest prayer you can offer."

Sarah reached over and tucked a strand of hair behind Brianna's ear, her touch gentle and warm. "You can be scared and still be held, Bree. You can be furious and still be loved. You can doubt everything you thought you knew and still be walking toward truth. They're not mutually exclusive."

"But what if I lose my faith completely? What if the questions are bigger than the answers?"

Her mother smiled, and for the first time that afternoon, it reached her eyes. "Then you'll be in very good company. Some of the most faithful people I know are the ones who've wrestled with the hardest questions and refused to settle for comfortable lies."

She gestured to the scattered photos around them—christenings and baptisms, youth group retreats and mission trips, the documentary evidence of a life lived in faith community. "This isn't about having perfect belief, honey. It's about showing up. It's about refusing to stop loving even when love breaks your heart. It's about trusting that the questions themselves are sacred, that the searching is part of what makes us human."

Brianna had nodded then, not fully understanding but sensing the importance of what her mother was trying to give her. It felt like receiving a road map for a journey she hadn't yet begun, instructions for navigating territory she couldn't yet imagine needing to cross.

"Will you remember this?" Sarah asked, gathering the photos into careful piles. "When things get hard—and they will get hard, because that's what life is—will you remember that doubt doesn't make you faithless? That questions don't make you broken?"

"I'll remember," Brianna promised, the words feeling like a vow though she didn't understand their full weight.

Now, sitting in Professor Martinez's classroom as he droned on about economic collapse and recovery, Brianna understood that her mother had been trying to prepare her. Somehow, Sarah had known that her daughter would need those words, that the comfortable certainty of teenage faith wouldn't survive what was coming. She had planted seeds on purpose, knowing they would need time to grow in dark soil before they could bloom.

You can be scared and still be held.

The words echoed in her memory with startling clarity, her mother's voice as real as if she were sitting in the desk beside her. For months, Brianna had treated her fear and her grief as proof that she'd been abandoned, that faith was a childhood fantasy she'd finally outgrown. But what if her mother had been right? What if being terrified didn't mean she had to be alone with her terror?

The professor's voice faded to background noise as Brianna sat with the revolutionary possibility that her anger and doubt weren't signs of spiritual failure but evidence that she was still engaged in the very wrestling her mother had described. She thought of her savage essay about Hopkins, the months of cynical philosophy with Liam, the walls she'd built against anyone who might offer comfort. All of it had felt like brave intellectual honesty, but maybe it had just been a more sophisticated form of running away.

Sometimes anger is the most honest prayer you can offer.

What if her fury at God wasn't blasphemy but conversation? What if her refusal to accept easy answers wasn't faithlessness but the very kind of faith her mother had tried to describe—the kind that demanded truth even when truth was complicated and painful?

The bell rang, startling her back to the present. Students around her were packing up their books, chattering about weekend plans and upcoming midterms. Brianna remained seated for a moment, letting the memory settle into her bones like medicine she'd finally learned how to swallow.

Walking back to her dorm through the golden afternoon light, she found herself thinking about seeds. How they had to be buried in darkness before they could grow. How the very thing that seemed like death—being covered in soil, cut off from light—was actually the condition necessary for new life.

Her mother's words had been planted two years ago in the safety of an ordinary Saturday afternoon. They had waited through the diagnosis and the treatments, through the long nights in hospital waiting rooms, through the funeral and the aftermath. They had survived her rejection of faith, her months of cynicism, her desperate attempts to build a life from pure reason and anger. And now, when she was finally ready to hear them, they were blooming in her memory like flowers she'd forgotten she'd been given.

Back in her room, Maya was at her desk working on an essay, surrounded by the organized chaos of research materials and color-coded notes. She looked up when Brianna entered, her expression shifting from concentration to gentle concern.

"You look like you've seen a ghost," Maya observed. "Everything okay?"

Brianna sat heavily on her bed, still processing the vividness of the memory. "Not a ghost exactly. More like... I remembered something my mom told me once. About doubt and faith and how they don't have to be enemies."

Maya set down her pen, giving Brianna her full attention. "What did she say?"

"That being angry at God isn't the same as not believing in God. That questions don't make you broken." Brianna looked across the room at her roommate, this girl who had somehow managed to hold onto hope despite her own experiences with loss. "I think I've been running from the wrong thing."

"What do you mean?"

"I thought I was running from God because He failed me. But maybe I was just running from a version of God that was too small for what I was experiencing. Maybe I was angry at my own expectations instead of... instead of whatever God actually is."

Maya nodded slowly, understanding flickering in her eyes. "It's scary when your picture of God gets too small to hold your real life."

"Yeah." Brianna pulled her knees up, unconsciously mirroring the position her mother had taken in the memory. "I don't know what comes next. I'm not ready to go back to church or start praying again or any of that. But I'm starting to think maybe... maybe I don't have to choose between being honest about how much this hurts and still believing that Someone is listening."

"Maybe that's exactly the kind of faith worth having," Maya said gently. "The kind that's big enough for all of it—the love and the loss and the questions and the anger. The kind that doesn't require you to pretend everything is fine in order to deserve comfort."

That evening, as Brianna tried to focus on her homework, she found her thoughts returning again and again to that golden afternoon two years ago. Her mother's voice, her touch, the careful way she had tried to prepare her daughter for a journey she wouldn't be able to make alongside her. It was a gift that had taken months to unwrap, instructions she'd had to grow into understanding.

She wasn't ready to call it prayer yet, but as she sat in the gathering darkness of her dorm room, holding the weight of her questions and her stubborn, reluctant hope, she felt something she hadn't experienced in months: the possibility of not being alone. Not because her pain had been taken away or her questions answered, but because the very act of wrestling with them might itself be a form of connection—with her mother's memory, with her own deepest self, and maybe, just maybe, with whatever divine presence was large enough to hold her fury without being diminished by it.

Outside, the evening bells began to ring across campus, their bronze voices carrying the same message they had offered for generations to students wrestling with their own versions of doubt and faith and the complicated work of growing up. For the first time in months, Brianna didn't flinch at the sound. She just listened, letting it remind her that some conversations were large enough to span lifetimes, that some seeds planted in love could survive even the harshest winters, waiting for the right moment to push through the dark soil and reach toward whatever light was still possible in a broken world.

The bells faded into the October evening, leaving behind a silence that felt expectant rather than empty. Brianna pulled out her phone, staring at the contact labeled "Dad" for a long moment before pressing call. It rang three times before his familiar voice answered, cautious in the way it had become since their conversations turned into careful negotiations around her grief.

"Bree? Everything okay?"

"It's Brianna, Dad," she said automatically, but the correction felt less sharp than usual, more like an old habit than a necessary defense. "And yeah. I'm okay. I was just... thinking about Mom today."

A pause on the other end, filled with the kind of careful stillness that came from months of learning which conversational paths were safe to walk down. "Oh. Good thoughts or...?"

"Good ones, actually." The words surprised her as she said them. "Remember that day she spent reorganizing all the photo albums? When I was sixteen? She told me all this stuff about faith and doubt that I didn't really understand then."

"I remember." His voice warmed slightly. "She came downstairs afterward and said she'd had an important conversation with you. Wouldn't tell me what it was about—said it was 'mother-daughter wisdom' and I'd have to wait for the footnotes."

The image of her parents in their kitchen, her mother protective of the sacred space she'd created with her daughter, made something tight in Brianna's chest loosen. "She was trying to prepare me, I think. For when things got hard."

"That sounds like your mom. She was always three steps ahead, trying to give you what you'd need before you knew you needed it." David's voice carried the particular mixture of love and loss that had become the soundtrack to their conversations about Sarah. "Did it help? What she told you?"

Brianna considered the question, thinking about the months of anger and the fortress of cynicism she'd built, the way her mother's words had waited patiently beneath all of that until she was ready to hear them. "Not right away. But maybe that was the point. Maybe some gifts have to age before they're useful."

"She always said you were too smart for easy answers," David said, and there was pride in his voice that Brianna hadn't heard in months. "Said you'd have to wrestle with the big questions yourself, and all she could do was make sure you had good wrestling partners."

"Is that what she called them? Wrestling partners?"

"Doubt, questions, anger—all of it. She said they weren't your enemies, they were your teachers. And that faith that couldn't survive a good fight wasn't worth much anyway."

The conversation felt different from their recent exchanges—less like two people carefully avoiding landmines and more like a father and daughter remembering someone they both loved. Brianna found herself thinking about the photo her mother had held that afternoon, the confirmation picture that had captured a moment of certainty neither of them could have known would become so complicated.

"Dad? Are you angry at God?"

The question hung in the air between them, heavy with months of unspoken honesty. When David finally answered, his voice was quieter, more vulnerable than she'd heard it since the funeral.

"Every day," he admitted. "I wake up and I'm furious that she's gone. That all her plans for the future just... stopped. That I have to figure out how to live without her while she's missing everything." His voice caught slightly. "But then I remember what she used to say about anger being another language for love, and I think maybe God can handle it. If He can't, what kind of God is He?"

It was an echo of Maya's words, of Dr. Finch's gentle wisdom, of her mother's prophetic preparation for this exact moment. The idea that God might be large enough to hold their fury without being diminished by it, patient enough to wait while they learned to trust again.

"I'm not ready to go back to church yet," Brianna said. "But I'm starting to think maybe I don't have to choose between being angry and being faithful."

"I don't think your mom would want you to go back to anything," David said. "I think she'd want you to go forward to something new. Something that's big enough for all of who you are now, not just who you were before."

After they hung up, Brianna sat in the darkening room, feeling the weight of connections she'd thought were broken beginning to weave back together in new patterns. Not the simple faith of her childhood, but something more complex and honest—a way of believing that could hold both her love for her mother and her fury at losing her, both her desire for answers and her growing acceptance that some questions might be sacred precisely because they couldn't be easily resolved.

Maya returned from the library as Brianna was getting ready for bed, her arms full of textbooks and her face showing the particular exhaustion that came from wrestling with organic chemistry equations. She glanced at Brianna, seeming to notice something different in the atmosphere of the room.

"You look peaceful," Maya observed, dropping her bag by her desk. "Not happy exactly, but... settled somehow."

"I talked to my dad tonight. Really talked to him, for the first time in months." Brianna pulled her hair into a loose ponytail, meeting Maya's eyes in the mirror above their shared dresser. "Turns out we're both angry at God. And we're both okay with that, maybe for the first time."

Maya smiled, the kind of understanding expression that came from her own experience with the complicated geography of faith and loss. "That sounds like progress."

"It feels like it," Brianna agreed. "Maya? That thing you mentioned about your ministry group—The Well? I'm still not ready for anything formal, but maybe... maybe I could come sit in sometime? Just to see what it's like?"

"Of course," Maya said, her voice carefully neutral despite the hope that flickered in her eyes. "No pressure, no agenda. Just people figuring things out together."

That night, Brianna dreamed of her mother's garden—not the way it had looked during the illness, with weeds creeping in at the edges, but the way it had been in its full glory. Row upon row of vegetables and flowers, everything growing exactly where it had been planted, but wild and abundant in the way that suggested both careful tending and trust in forces beyond human control.

In the dream, her mother was kneeling in the soil, her hands dirty with the work of planting seeds she wouldn't live to see bloom. But she was smiling, humming one of those old hymns under her breath, completely absorbed in the ancient act of burial that preceded resurrection.

"Some things have to die before they can really live," dream-Sarah said without looking up, her voice carrying across the garden like a blessing Brianna was finally ready to receive. "But that doesn't mean they're really gone. It just means they're getting ready to surprise you."

Brianna woke with tears on her cheeks, but for the first time in months, they weren't tears of despair. They were the kind that came from recognizing a gift you hadn't known you'd been given, from understanding that love could be stronger than loss even when loss had the last word.

Outside, the campus was beginning to stir with the sounds of another Thursday morning—students hurrying to early classes, the distant rumble of maintenance trucks, the ordinary rhythms of a community going about its daily work of learning and growing and becoming. She lay in bed listening to it all, no longer feeling separate from the life happening around her, but not yet fully ready to rejoin it either.

She was in between, suspended in that liminal space where old certainties had crumbled but new ones hadn't yet formed. It was uncomfortable territory, but it was honest territory. And for the first time since her mother's death, honest felt like something she could build a life on.

The day ahead held the usual obligations—classes and assignments and the ongoing work of being a college student. But it also held possibility she hadn't allowed herself to feel in months. The possibility that her questions might be sacred, that her anger might be prayer, that the faith she'd thought was dead might simply be transforming into something large enough to hold all the complicated truths of her actual life.

She thought of her mother's hands in the dream garden, planting seeds with such confidence and care despite not knowing exactly what would grow from them. It was an act of faith that had nothing to do with certainty and everything to do with love—love patient enough to work in darkness, trust deep enough to let go of control over outcomes.

Maybe, Brianna thought as she finally rose to meet the day, that was what resurrection looked like. Not the dramatic return of what had been lost, but the slow, surprising emergence of something new from the fertile soil of what had been buried with such careful attention to the possibility of hope.

Chapter Ten

The Cup of Tea

The week after brunch passed in a strange suspension, like living inside a snow globe that someone had shaken and was waiting to settle. Brianna moved through her classes with a new awareness of the space between her old self and whoever she was becoming—too far from the bitter fortress she'd built to retreat completely, but not yet brave enough to step fully into the light Maya and her friends had offered.

She caught herself doing small things differently. Responding to her father's texts with actual words—*How was your day?* instead of *Fine*—and sometimes even adding a heart emoji that felt both foreign and warm against her fingertips. Sitting closer to the front in Dr. Finch's class instead of hiding in the back row, close enough to ask a question about the reading instead of letting confusion wash over her in silence. Making eye contact with the barista at the campus coffee shop and remembering her name was Maya, accepting the extra foam art she offered with a small smile instead of staring at her phone screen like a shield.

And then there was the green sweater—soft wool the color of new leaves that her mother had folded carefully in tissue paper last Christmas. She found herself reaching for it instead of defaulting to her armor of black and gray, the way she'd been reaching for shadows. The green felt like choosing warmth over numbness, like stepping into sunlight after months underground. It meant wearing something her mother had touched with love instead of wrapping herself in colors that matched the hollow spaces inside her chest.

She started leaving her dorm room door cracked open when she studied, no longer sealing herself away completely. Bought fresh fruit at the market instead of surviving on vending machine meals. Let herself laugh—actually laugh—when her roommate told a terrible joke, the sound surprising them both.

None of it felt revolutionary—just quiet shifts, tectonic plates moving so slowly she could almost convince herself they weren't moving at all. But they were. From surviving toward something that whispered of living.

Maya seemed to sense the change too, though she was careful not to name it. Their conversations grew longer, less guarded. Maya shared stories about her friends from brunch, her struggles with organic chemistry, the way she missed her family's Sunday dinners. In return, Brianna found herself offering small pieces of her own story—not the big, terrible center of it, but the edges where it was safe to let someone else look.

It was Thursday evening when the first real crack appeared in the careful distance Brianna had maintained.

She was sitting at her desk, staring at a blank document that was supposed to become a paper on Dickinson's use of dashes, when the familiar tightness began in her chest. It started as it always did—the sharp, sweet sting of *L'Occitane Lavender* hand lotion cutting through the stale library air like a blade. Her lungs seized. The scent dragged her back instantly: her mother's cool palms cupping her fevered cheeks during childhood flu, those same gentle fingers working through tangles in her hair before school pictures, the careful way she'd smooth down Brianna's cowlick with lavender-scented hands that smelled of comfort and safety. The phantom sensation hit her like a physical blow—her mother's soft fingertips tracing her hairline, the slight callus on her thumb from years of gardening, the warmth that used to seep into Brianna's scalp. Then came the crushing, breathless recognition that slammed into her chest and spread outward like poison: those hands were ash now. Those fingers would never braid her hair again, never check her forehead for fever, never exist anywhere but in the merciless precision of memory. The laptop screen blurred. Her fingers went numb on the keyboard.

But this time, instead of the clean, intellectual anger she'd learned to summon, or the numbing cynicism that had been her refuge, something rawer surfaced. The grief she'd been holding at arm's length for months broke through her defenses like water through a cracked dam, and suddenly she couldn't breathe around the weight of it.

She pressed her palms against her eyes, trying to push the tears back, but they came anyway—not the bitter tears of rage or the empty tears of exhaustion, but something deeper. Something that felt like it was being pulled from her bones.

"Hey," Maya's voice was soft, careful. "You okay?"

Brianna looked up, her vision blurred, to find her roommate watching her with concern that held no judgment, no demand for explanation. Just presence, the kind that didn't require words to communicate care.

"I'm fine," Brianna started automatically, but the lie crumbled before it could fully form. "No. I'm not fine. I'm... I miss her so much I can't breathe sometimes."

The admission hung in the air between them, naked and vulnerable in a way Brianna hadn't allowed herself to be since the funeral. She waited for Maya to offer some cliché, to suggest prayer or positive thinking or any of the hollow comforts people usually reached for in the face of someone else's pain.

Instead, Maya just nodded. "That sounds exhausting."

The simple validation—not an attempt to fix or minimize, just acknowledgment of how hard it was to carry that kind of missing—undid something in Brianna's chest. The tears came harder now, and with them, words she hadn't been able to speak aloud.

"She was supposed to see me graduate. She was supposed to help me move into my first apartment and meet whoever I was going to marry and hold her grandchildren. She had all these plans, all these things she was looking forward to, and now she's just... gone. And everyone keeps telling me she's in a better place, but I don't care if it's better. I want her here."

Maya moved quietly to her mini-fridge and pulled out a bottle of water, setting it on Brianna's desk without fanfare. Then she sat on her own bed, close enough to be present but far enough away to give Brianna space to fall apart without feeling crowded.

"Of course you want her here," Maya said quietly. "She was your person. The fact that you miss her this much—it's not a problem to be solved. It's proof of how much love you carried for each other."

The words were so different from everything Brianna had heard over the past months—the suggestions that she needed to "move through" her grief, that dwelling on her loss was unhealthy, that she should focus on the "gift" of her mother's life instead of the tragedy of her death. Maya wasn't trying to redirect her pain or reframe it as something more palatable. She was simply sitting with it, allowing it to exist without needing to be transformed into something else.

"I don't know how to do this," Brianna whispered. "I don't know how to live in a world where she doesn't exist."

"You don't have to figure it all out tonight," Maya said. "You don't have to figure it out tomorrow, either. You just have to keep breathing, one breath at a time, until breathing gets a little easier. And then a little easier after that."

It was the same advice her mother might have given, practical and gentle and free of false promises. Brianna reached for the water bottle Maya had left for her, her hands shaking slightly as she twisted off the cap.

"I used to pray every night that God would save her," she continued, the words spilling out now that the dam had broken. "Even after the doctors said there was nothing more they could do, I kept believing that if I just had enough faith, if I prayed hard enough, He would perform a miracle. And when she died, I felt like such a fool. Like I'd been talking to myself in an empty room for two years."

Maya was quiet for a long moment, and when she spoke, her voice carried its own weight of experience. "When my aunt was dying, I did the same thing. Bargained with God, promised I'd be a better person, begged for more time. When she died, I was so angry I couldn't even say grace at dinner for months. My mom kept asking if I wanted to talk to Pastor Williams, and I wanted to scream at her that Pastor Williams had never watched someone he loved disappear piece by piece while God did nothing."

The shared recognition—that Maya had walked through her own valley of anger and doubt—made Brianna feel less alone in a way she hadn't expected. Not because Maya's loss made her own smaller, but because it proved that the questions she was wrestling with were human ones, not character flaws or failures of faith.

"What changed?" Brianna asked. "I mean, you still believe in something, right? You go to that ministry group."

Maya smiled, but it was complicated, shadowed with memory. "I think I had to learn the difference between the vending machine God I'd been sold and the God I was actually encountering in the mess of real life. The God of my childhood was supposed to be transactional—put in enough prayer and good behavior, get out protection and answered requests. That

God was meant to shield the faithful from suffering, to make everything work out according to some divine plan that always made sense if you just had enough faith.

When that cosmic butler didn't show up—when good people still got cancer, when prayers seemed to hit the ceiling, when the world felt random and brutal—I assumed it meant the whole thing was a lie. But what I discovered, through years of wrestling and rage and doubt, was something harder to grasp but more honest: a God who doesn't prevent the storm but shows up *in* it. Not the God who gives easy answers, but the one who sits with you in the questions. I had to learn that faith could include fury, that you could shake your fist at heaven and still be in relationship with the divine. The God I found wasn't smaller than my childhood version—just more willing to get their hands dirty in the actual human experience."

She pulled her knees up to her chest, wrapping her arms around them in a gesture that made her look younger, more vulnerable. "But then I started noticing the people who showed up when God didn't. The nurses who worked extra shifts to sit with my aunt when we couldn't be there. The neighbor who brought groceries every week without being asked. My friend Katie who let me cry on her shoulder for months without ever telling me I needed to get over it. And I started wondering if maybe that was God too—not the cosmic fixer I'd been praying to, but something quieter. Something that worked through human hands and voices and presence."

It was a different way of thinking about faith than anything Brianna had encountered—not as a set of beliefs to be defended or rejected, but as an ongoing relationship with mystery that could include doubt and anger and still somehow remain sacred.

"I don't know if I'm ready for that," Brianna said honestly. "The God part, I mean. I'm still too angry."

"Anger might be the most honest prayer you can offer right now," Maya said. "God can handle it. If He can't, He's not much of a God anyway."

They sat in comfortable quiet for a while, the only sounds the hum of the heating system and the distant murmur of students in the hallway. Brianna felt wrung out but oddly peaceful, like a storm that had finally blown itself out, leaving the air clean and still in its wake.

"Maya?" she said eventually.

"Yeah?"

"Thank you. For not trying to fix me. For just... being here."

Maya's smile was soft and real. "Thank you for letting me. And Brianna? You don't need to be fixed. You just need to be heard."

Later that night, after Maya had turned off her desk lamp and settled into sleep, Brianna lay awake staring at the ceiling. The conversation had shifted something fundamental in how she understood her own grief—not as a problem to be solved or a weakness to be overcome, but as a natural response to profound loss, deserving of patience rather than judgment.

She thought about Maya's words—that anger might be the most honest prayer she could offer. The idea felt both terrifying and liberating. If her fury at God was actually a form of communication rather than blasphemy, then maybe she hadn't lost her faith entirely. Maybe she'd just been speaking a different language than she was used to.

She wasn't ready to call it prayer yet. But for the first time in months, she could imagine a version of herself that might someday be able to sit with both her questions and her hope, her anger and her love, without needing to choose between them.

It was a small beginning, fragile as new growth, but it was hers. And in the quiet darkness of their shared room, with Maya's gentle breathing as a counterpoint to her thoughts, it felt like enough.

In the morning, there would be classes and assignments and the ongoing work of figuring out who she was becoming. But tonight, there was just the peace of having been seen and accepted in her broken state, the radical gift of unconditional presence that asked nothing in return.

Outside their window, the campus was settling into its late-night quiet, students tucked away in dorms and apartments across the small college town. Somewhere in that constellation of lit windows, other people were probably wrestling with their own versions of doubt and loss and the complicated work of growing up.

The thought should have made her feel small, insignificant in the face of so much shared human struggle. Instead, it made her feel connected to something larger than her individual pain—part of a community of people trying to make sense of love and loss and the mystery of what it meant to keep hoping when hope felt dangerous.

Maya had offered her water when she was crying, presence when she was falling apart, space to be angry without judgment. It was such a small thing, really—being kind to someone who was hurting. But in a world that often demanded performance and gratitude and quick healing, Maya's simple act of witness felt revolutionary.

Brianna pulled her covers up to her chin and let her eyes drift closed. Tomorrow, she would continue the slow work of learning to live with her loss. But tonight, she was held by the knowledge that she didn't have to do it alone, that there were people in the world who could sit with pain without trying to take it away, who understood that sometimes the deepest healing happened not through fixing, but through faithful presence.

It was the kind of love her mother would have recognized—practical, patient, and utterly without conditions. The kind that didn't promise to make everything better, but promised not to leave you alone in the dark.

And for now, that was enough.

Chapter Eleven

The Empathy of the Sage

Dr. Finch's office hours on Tuesday afternoon felt like stepping into a different season. The October light slanting through his tall windows had turned golden and thick, catching the dust motes that danced between towers of books like tiny prayers made visible. The familiar smell of pipe tobacco and old paper wrapped around Brianna as she knocked on the heavy oak door, no longer a fortress to be breached but simply the workspace of a man who had learned to live with difficult questions.

"Come in," his voice rumbled from within, and when she pushed the door open, he looked up from a stack of papers with that same quiet attention that had once felt like a threat. Now it just felt like being seen.

"Brianna," he said, setting down his pen. "I was hoping you'd stop by. Please, sit."

She settled into the worn leather chair across from his desk, the same seat where she'd once felt so exposed and defensive. Today, the vulnerability felt different—not like something being done to her, but something she was choosing to carry into this space.

"I wanted to talk about my essay," she said, then paused, correcting herself. "Actually, I wanted to talk about what you said. About Hopkins. About anger being love with nowhere to go."

Dr. Finch leaned back in his chair, his fingers steepled in front of him. "Ah. And what did you think of that notion, now that you've had some time to sit with it?"

The question was gentle, genuinely curious rather than leading. Brianna found herself thinking of Maya's words from the night before—that anger might be the most honest prayer she could offer.

"I think," she said carefully, "that I've been trying to choose between being angry and being faithful. Like they were opposite things. But maybe they're not?"

"Tell me more about that."

She looked out the window, watching students cross the quad with their backpacks and their certainties, their easy laughter carrying on the autumn air. "I loved my mother more than anything in the world. When she got sick, I prayed harder than I'd ever prayed for anything. I believed—really believed—that God would save her if I just had enough faith." Her voice caught slightly. "And when He didn't, I felt betrayed. Not just sad, but personally betrayed. Like I'd been lied to."

Dr. Finch nodded slowly. "That sounds like a reasonable response to a promise that felt broken."

"But that's just it—was it a promise? Or was that just what I wanted to believe?" She turned back to face him. "I've been so angry at God for not being who I thought He was. But what if I was angry at the wrong thing? What if I was angry at my own expectations instead of... instead of whatever God actually is?"

The distinction felt important, though she couldn't quite articulate why. Dr. Finch seemed to understand the weight of what she was wrestling with.

"In my experience," he said quietly, "the God worth getting angry at is rarely the God we construct in our minds. The God of our expectations is usually too small for our fury. But the God who can hold our rage, who can sit with us in it without being diminished—that's a God large enough to be worth wrestling with."

"Like Jacob," Brianna said, the reference surfacing from some half-remembered Sunday school lesson. "Wrestling with the angel until daybreak."

"Exactly. Jacob demanded a blessing from the very being who had wounded him. He wouldn't let go until he received it. That's not the action of someone who has lost faith—that's the action of someone whose faith is strong enough to demand answers."

The idea settled into her chest like a key finding its lock. She thought of the months she'd spent trying to convince herself she didn't believe anymore, the energy she'd put into building intellectual arguments against God's existence. If she truly believed there was nothing there, why had she worked so hard to disprove it? Why had the silence hurt so much if she didn't still, somewhere deep down, believe someone was supposed to be listening?

"I don't know how to have that kind of faith," she admitted. "The wrestling kind. It seems so... messy."

Dr. Finch's smile was warm and knowing. "Faith that can't survive messiness isn't faith—it's wishful thinking. Real faith, the kind that lasts, is forged in the very mess you're afraid of. It's not about having all the answers. It's about being brave enough to keep asking the questions."

He pulled a slim volume from one of the stacks on his desk and held it out to her. "Hopkins again. But this time, not just his dark night of the soul. Read 'The Windhover'—see what happened when he learned to find God not in spite of the struggle, but in the very heart of it."

Brianna took the book, its cover worn soft from countless hands seeking the same understanding she was grappling with. "Dr. Finch? Can I ask you something personal?"

"Of course."

"When your son died—did you really find your way back to believing? Or are you still wrestling?"

His expression grew thoughtful, distant. "Both," he said finally. "Some days I wake up certain that love is the fundamental force of the universe, that death is not the final word. Other days, I can barely get out of bed because the silence feels so absolute." He looked directly at her, his eyes carrying the weight of his own losses. "But I've learned that faith isn't a destination you arrive at and then get to rest. It's a muscle you have to keep exercising, especially when it hurts to use it."

"And the anger?"

"Still there," he said simply. "But it's not the acid it used to be. Now it's more like... refined fire. It burns away what isn't essential and leaves behind what is. The love I had for my son. The hope that there's meaning in the connection we shared. The stubborn belief that a universe capable of producing that kind of love can't be entirely random."

Brianna felt something shift in her understanding—not a sudden revelation, but a slow realignment, like a photograph coming into focus. Her anger at God wasn't evidence that her faith was dead. It was evidence that it was still alive, still demanding to be reckoned with.

"I'm not ready to pray yet," she said. "Not in the way I used to."

"What if prayer isn't what you used to think it was?" Dr. Finch suggested. "What if it's not about asking for things or even praising? What if it's simply the act of showing up with your whole self—doubt, anger, questions and all—and trusting that someone is listening, even in the silence?"

The conversation stayed with her as she walked back across campus, the Hopkins collection tucked under her arm like a map to territory she wasn't sure she was ready to explore. The afternoon light was beginning to fade, students streaming toward the dining hall with their easy chatter about midterms and weekend plans. She felt separate from their certainties, but no longer in a way that felt like exile. More like she was walking a different path that occasionally intersected with theirs.

Back in her room, Maya was at her desk with her organic chemistry textbook, muttering under her breath about molecular structures. She looked up when Brianna entered.

"How was office hours?" Maya asked, then seemed to hear how that sounded. "Sorry, you don't have to tell me. I'm just curious because you looked... I don't know, lighter somehow when you left."

Brianna settled onto her bed, the Hopkins book in her lap. "He gave me something to read. About wrestling with faith instead of trying to perfect it."

"That sounds very Dr. Finch," Maya said with a smile. "He's good at meeting people where they are instead of where he thinks they should be."

"Maya? Can I ask you something?"

"Always."

"When you pray—do you ever get angry? Like, in the middle of praying?"

Maya set down her highlighter, considering the question seriously. "All the time. Sometimes I start praying and end up basically yelling at God about how unfair everything is. I used to think that made me a bad Christian. Now I think it just makes me honest."

"Do you think God minds?"

"I think God would rather have our real feelings than our polite perfor-mance," Maya said. "Even if our real feelings are messy and demanding and not very holy-sounding."

That evening, Brianna opened the Hopkins collection to "The Wind-hover." The poem was dense, difficult, full of language that seemed to fold in on itself. But as she read it again and again, something began to emerge—not the tortured questioning of his dark sonnets, but a kind of fierce joy, a recognition of beauty so intense it felt like prayer made visible.

I caught this morning morning's minion, king-dom of daylight's dauphin, dapple-dawn-drawn Falcon, in his riding Of the rolling level underneath him steady air...

She could see it—the bird suspended in perfect flight, mastering the wind not by fighting it but by dancing with it, finding grace in the very elements that could destroy it. And in the final lines, the transformation that took her breath away:

...blue-bleak embers, ah my dear, Fall, gall themselves, and gash gold-ver-million.

Even the dying coals, when they broke open, revealed fire at their core. Even destruction could be a form of revelation, if you had eyes to see it.

Brianna closed the book and sat in the gathering darkness of their room, something new stirring in her chest. Not certainty—she was still too raw for that. But possibility. The recognition that her breaking might not be the end of her story, but the very thing that allowed light to pour in.

She wasn't ready to call it prayer yet. But as she sat there in the quiet, holding the weight of her questions and her anger and her stubborn, reluc-tant hope, she could almost imagine that someone was listening. Someone large enough to hold her fury without being diminished by it, patient enough to wait while she learned to trust again, loving enough to meet her exactly where she was instead of where she thought she should be.

Outside, the evening bells began to ring, their bronze voices carrying across the campus like an ancient conversation between earth and sky. For the first time in months, Brianna didn't flinch at the sound. She just listened, letting it wash over her like a blessing she was finally ready to receive.

The bells faded into the October evening, leaving behind a silence that felt different from the hollow quiet Brianna had grown accustomed to. This wasn't the absence of sound—it was the presence of peace, fragile but real, settling over the campus like the first snow of winter.

She stood and walked to the window, pressing her palm against the cool glass. Below, students moved along the lit pathways, their voices carrying fragments of conversation—complaints about professors, excitement about weekend plans, the easy intimacies of people who still believed the world made sense. Once, their certainty had felt like an accusation. Now it just seemed like a different season of life, one she might return to someday, changed but not broken by her journey through the darker months.

Maya's desk lamp clicked on, casting its warm circle of light across scattered chemistry notes. "I'm making tea," Maya said quietly. "Want some?"

The question was simple, domestic, offered without weight or expectation. But Brianna heard in it an echo of every small kindness Maya had extended over the past months—the cups of chamomile left on her nightstand, the space held open for her to be angry or sad or confused without judgment. Each gesture had been a thread, and now she could see the net Maya had woven beneath her, so quietly and patiently that Brianna hadn't noticed she was being caught.

"Yes," Brianna said. "I'd like that."

As Maya busied herself with the electric kettle and two mismatched mugs, Brianna opened the Hopkins book again, this time to one of the later poems. The words swam before her eyes at first, dense with Victorian syntax and Gerard Manley Hopkins' particular way of wrestling language into submission. But gradually, something emerged—not answers, but better questions. Not certainty, but the courage to keep seeking.

The tea was chamomile again, fragrant with honey Maya had stirred in without asking if she wanted it sweetened. They sat in comfortable quiet, two college students drinking tea and studying on a Tuesday night, the ordinariness of it precious after so many months of extraordinary pain.

"Maya?" Brianna said eventually.

"Mm?"

"I think I might want to go back to The Well sometime. Not this Sunday, but... maybe soon."

Maya's smile was careful, hopeful but not pushing. "They'd be glad to see you. No pressure, though. Whenever you're ready."

"I know." Brianna took another sip of tea, letting its warmth settle into her bones. "I'm starting to think maybe ready isn't something you wait to become. Maybe it's something you choose to be, even when you're scared."

Outside, a late owl called from the old oak tree by the library, its voice lonely but not despairing. Somewhere in the distance, she could hear laughter from an open dorm window, the rise and fall of friends sharing the kind of moment that would become a memory they'd carry long after graduation.

The Hopkins book lay open beside her, its pages filled with the testimony of a man who had learned to find God not in the absence of struggle, but in its very center. Tomorrow there would be classes and assignments and the ongoing work of learning to live with questions that might never have clean answers. But tonight, there was tea and companionship and the radical possibility that her story was still being written, one word at a time, one breath at a time, one small act of faith at a time.

For the first time in longer than she could remember, that felt like enough.

Chapter Twelve

The Terror of the Void

The midpoint arrived not with fanfare but with the sickening lurch of certainty suddenly questioned. It was a Thursday night in early November, the kind of evening when autumn finally admitted it was dying and winter pressed its face against the windows like an unwelcome visitor. Brianna had been making progress—small, tentative steps toward something that felt like healing rather than just survival. She'd had coffee with Imani from Maya's group, spent an hour looking at paintings that found beauty in ruins. She'd called her father twice without being prompted, conversations that felt less like obligations and more like the careful reconstruction of a bridge. She'd even attended one of Dr. Finch's evening lectures on faith in modern poetry, sitting in the back but actually listening instead of building walls with her laptop screen.

The progress felt real, substantial. She was sleeping better, eating meals that weren't just caffeine and spite, allowing herself to wear colors that weren't exclusively drawn from the palette of grief. Maya had mentioned The Well again—not pushing, just keeping the door open—and Brianna had found herself actually considering it instead of reflexively recoiling.

Which made what happened at Sigma Chi all the more devastating.

She hadn't planned to go. Thursday evening stretched before her like a sanctuary—homework spread across her desk, perhaps a movie with

Maya, the sort of quiet ritual that had grown sacred through months of reconstruction. But when Imani texted about a friend's birthday, something newly awakened in Brianna—something weary of perpetual caution—whispered *yes* before her careful, guarded self could silence it.

The healing had been tentative but real. Small gestures toward light: accepting invitations, returning calls, allowing herself to believe that connection might not always lead to devastation. Progress measured in breaths taken freely, in laughter that came without calculation. She was learning, slowly, to trust the ground beneath her feet again.

She should have known better than to trust it completely.

"You sure?" Maya had asked, looking up from her organic chemistry textbook with the kind of gentle concern that never felt like judgment. "You've been doing so well with the whole... taking care of yourself thing."

"It's just a few hours," Brianna had said, pulling on the green sweater her mother had chosen, the one that had become her uniform of tentative hope. "I'll be back before midnight, like some kind of reverse Cinderella."

The party was exactly what she should have expected—loud music bleeding through thin walls, the sticky-sweet smell of spilled beer and desperate perfume, students performing their Friday night selves with Thursday night energy. But there was something different about experiencing it now, after months of stepping back from the noise. The chaos that had once felt like liberation now just felt... hollow. Performative. A room full of people desperately trying to convince each other they were having the time of their lives.

She was standing near the kitchen, nursing a beer she didn't really want, when she heard Liam's voice cutting through the music like a blade.

He was holding court near the back porch, surrounded by the usual collection of philosophy majors and creative writing students who treated cynicism like a competitive sport. His dark hair was longer now, falling across his forehead in a way that suggested studied carelessness, and he was wearing the same Nirvana t-shirt she remembered from their first conversation at the involvement fair. The one that had seemed authentic then and looked like a costume now.

"—the problem with most people," he was saying, his voice carrying that familiar blend of intellectual authority and casual cruelty that had once felt like wisdom, "is they're terrified of admitting that love is just evolutionary programming. They dress up biological imperatives in romantic language because the alternative—accepting that we're all just sophisticated animals following chemical commands—is too scary for their precious sense of meaning."

The girl beside him, young-looking even by college standards, was hanging on his every word with the kind of rapt attention Brianna remembered giving him during their late-night conversations at The Alibi. She had the same hungry look Brianna had once seen in her own mirror—someone desperate for a framework that made sense of the chaos, willing to trade wonder for certainty.

"But what about the feeling of it?" the girl asked, her voice tentative. "Like, when you really love someone, it feels like more than just chemistry, doesn't it?"

Liam's smile was sharp, predatory in a way Brianna had somehow managed to miss when she'd been the one receiving it. "Feelings are just stories we tell ourselves about our neurochemistry. Love, grief, hope—they're all just elaborate lies designed to make us feel special instead of acknowledging that we're cosmic accidents in a universe that doesn't give a hoot about our emotional narratives."

The words hit Brianna like a physical blow, not because they challenged her beliefs but because she recognized them so clearly. They were her words, or close enough—the gospel she'd preached to herself for months, the bitter comfort she'd wrapped around her grief like a blanket made of thorns. Hearing them in Liam's mouth, delivered with such casual cruelty to a girl who was clearly struggling, made her see them for what they actually were.

Not wisdom. Not intellectual honesty. Just sophisticated cruelty, dressed up in academic language.

"That seems..." the girl started, then stopped, her face falling as she processed the implications of what Liam was saying.

"Overwhelming?" Liam supplied. "Good. Truth usually is. Most people can't handle it, which is why they retreat into comforting fantasies about meaning and purpose and love that transcends biology. But once you accept the beautiful nihilism of it all, you're free. Free from expectations, free from disappointment, free from the exhausting work of caring about things that don't actually matter."

Free. The word that had once felt like salvation now sounded like the death rattle of everything that made life worth living. Brianna watched the girl's face crumple slightly, watched her retreat into herself as Liam's philosophy did what it was designed to do—strip away hope, connection, the messy, complicated, necessary work of being human.

This was what Brianna had looked like, she realized with growing horror. This was the expression she'd worn for months—not enlightenment, but devastation. Not freedom, but the hollow satisfaction of convincing herself that emptiness was preferable to the risk of being hurt again.

"Excuse me," she heard herself saying, stepping into the circle before she could think better of it. "I think you're wrong."

Liam's head turned, and his expression shifted through surprise, recognition, and something that looked almost like hunger. "Brianna," he said, his voice smooth as poisoned honey. "I wondered when you'd come back around. Ready to rejoin the ranks of the intellectually honest?"

The words were delivered with casual confidence, as if her return was inevitable, as if the months of growth and healing and tentative steps toward something better had been nothing more than a temporary detour. As if she belonged to him and his philosophy in some fundamental way that couldn't be changed by actual experience or genuine reflection.

"No," she said, surprised by how steady her voice sounded. "I came to tell you that your beautiful nihilism is bull."

The circle of students went quiet, sensing drama. Liam's eyebrows rose, his expression shifting to the amused condescension she remembered so well.

"Oh, this should be interesting," he said. "Please, enlighten us. What profound wisdom have you discovered in your journey back to comforting delusions?"

The mockery in his voice was designed to shut her down, to make her feel foolish for challenging the gospel of nothing he preached so eloquently. For a moment, she felt the old familiar shame rise in her throat—the sense that her hope was naive, her healing superficial, her tentative faith in goodness a sign of intellectual weakness.

But then she thought of Maya's quiet kindness, offered without agenda or expectation. Of Dr. Finch's patient empathy, his willingness to sit with her anger without trying to fix it. Of her father's lonely voice on the phone, admitting his own grief instead of performing strength. Of Imani's paintings, finding beauty in broken places not by denying the brokenness but by celebrating what grew from it.

"I learned that nihilism isn't brave," she said, her voice growing stronger. "It's the most cowardly philosophy there is. It's what you choose when you're too scared to risk believing in something that might hurt you."

Liam's expression hardened. "And what exactly do you believe in, Brianna? The same God who let your mother die? The same faith that failed you when you needed it most?"

It was a low blow, designed to send her retreating back into the familiar comfort of shared cynicism. The girl beside him looked uncomfortable now, as if she was beginning to see something ugly in the philosophy she'd been so eager to

"I believe in the people who showed up when God felt absent," Brianna said, the words coming from some deep well of truth she hadn't known she possessed. "I believe in the friend who left tea on my nightstand without being asked. In the professor who shared his own grief instead of trying to fix mine. In the father who admitted he was lost too instead of pretending he had answers. Those aren't evolutionary accidents or chemical tricks. They're choices. Choices to love and care and hope even when there's no guarantee it won't end in loss."

Liam's laugh was sharp, brittle at the edges. "How *quaint*. The grieving girl finds meaning in people bringing her beverages." His eyes swept the room, seeking allies among the other students. "This is exactly the kind of sentimental delusion I've been warning you about. Pain makes us desperate for fairy tales."

But something had shifted in Brianna's posture—a straightening, a settling into herself. "You want to know what's truly desperate, Liam? Building an entire worldview around the premise that caring is stupid. That's not philosophical sophistication—that's cowardice dressed up in big words."

"Cowardice?" His voice pitched higher, the practiced smoothness cracking. "I'm the one willing to face reality without—"

"Without what? Without risk?" Brianna stepped closer, and for the first time since she'd known him, Liam seemed to shrink. "Your nihilism isn't brave truth-telling. It's the ultimate hedge bet. If nothing matters, then you can never be wrong about what matters. If love is just chemistry, then you can never be hurt by its absence. If hope is delusion, then you never have to face the terror of hoping for something.

Liam's smirk nowhere to be found. "You don't understand the implications of what you're—"

"I understand perfectly." Her voice was gentle now, which somehow made it more devastating. "I understand that your Gospel of Nothing is just another way of avoiding the one question that actually matters: not whether life has inherent meaning, but whether you're brave enough to create meaning anyway. Whether you're brave enough to love people who will die, to hope for things that might not happen, to care about a world that doesn't guarantee it will care back."

She paused, looking directly into his eyes. "I've been where you are, Liam. Hiding behind intellectual superiority because it felt safer than admitting I was just scared and hurt and human. But that's not philosophy—that's just fear with footnotes."

"Sentiment," Liam dismissed, but there was something desperate in his voice now, as if her words were threatening the carefully constructed edifice of his worldview. "Pretty stories you're telling yourself to avoid facing reality."

"No," Brianna said, and she felt something shift inside her chest, something that had been slowly mending finally clicking into place. "They're the most real things I know. Your reality—where love is just chemistry and kindness is just programming—that's the story. That's the lie we tell ourselves when we're too afraid to risk being human."

She turned to the girl who'd been hanging on Liam's every word. "He's going to tell you that caring about anything is weakness. That hope is delusion. That the only honest way to live is to expect nothing and feel nothing and connect to nothing because it's all meaningless anyway." Her voice softened. "But I've lived in that world. It's not freedom. It's prison. And you don't have to choose it just because someone with a philosophy degree says it's intellectually superior."

The girl nodded slightly, something like relief flickering across her face. Around them, other students were listening now, drawn by the raw honesty of the exchange.

"You want to know what I think is intellectually superior?" Brianna continued, turning back to Liam. "Choosing love even when you know it ends. Choosing hope even when you've been disappointed. Choosing connection even when people leave. That takes courage. That takes strength. Your nihilism is just giving up and calling it wisdom."

For a moment, Liam's mask slipped, and she saw something vulnerable underneath—a flash of the scared, hurt boy who had built his entire identity around the philosophy of nothing because it felt safer than risking everything. But then the mask snapped back into place, and his smile turned cruel.

"How touching," he said. "I give you six months before reality breaks your heart again and you come crawling back to the truth. Some people need to touch the stove twice to learn it's hot."

It should have hurt. For months, his approval had been the thing she craved most, his philosophy the framework she'd used to make sense of her pain. His dismissal should have sent her spiraling back into doubt and self-recrimination.

Instead, she felt something like pity. For the boy who was so afraid of being hurt that he'd convinced himself feeling nothing was victory. For the philosophy that was so afraid of beauty it had to explain it away. For the worldview so terrified of meaning it had to systematically destroy every source of it.

"Maybe," she said quietly. "But at least I'll know I tried. At least I'll know I was brave enough to risk it."

She turned and walked away, leaving Liam and his circle of converts to their gospel of emptiness. Behind her, she could hear the conversation resuming, but quieter now, less certain. She'd planted a seed of doubt in the absolute certainty of nihilism, and that felt like enough.

The walk back to her dorm was clear and cold, November air sharp in her lungs like the breath of winter. Above her, stars wheeled in their ancient patterns, distant and cold but somehow not indifferent. They were just stars, following the laws of physics across a universe too vast to comprehend. But they were also beautiful. They were also the same lights that had guided travelers and inspired poets and made children wish for impossible things. Both things were true, and that truth felt like a revelation.

Back in her room, Maya looked up from her textbook with concern. "You're back early. Everything okay?"

Brianna sat on her bed, still processing what had happened. "I saw Liam," she said finally. "Had a conversation that was... clarifying."

"Good clarifying or bad clarifying?"

"Good, I think." Brianna pulled off her sweater, the soft green wool that had been her armor and her hope. "I realized I spent so much time being afraid of believing in the wrong things that I almost stopped believing in anything at all. But not believing—that's not protecting yourself. That's just... disappearing."

Maya set down her highlighter, giving Brianna her full attention. "What changed your mind?"

Brianna thought about the question seriously. "You," she said finally. "Dr. Finch. My dad. Everyone who chose to show up and care even when I was determined to push you away. You could have decided I wasn't worth the effort. But you kept leaving tea on my nightstand. You kept holding space for me to be angry or sad or confused without making me feel broken. That's not evolutionary programming. That's choice. That's love."

"That's faith," Maya added quietly.

"Yeah," Brianna said, the word feeling strange and familiar on her tongue. "I guess it is."

She pulled out her phone and scrolled to a contact she hadn't used in weeks. Her old youth pastor, Mike, who had been texting sporadically with messages she'd been too angry to answer. She typed carefully:

Hi Pastor Mike. I know I haven't been in touch. I've been struggling with faith and doubt and anger at God. But I'm learning that maybe struggling WITH faith is different from struggling WITHOUT it. Would it be okay if I called you sometime? I have questions, but they're different questions than before.

His response came back almost immediately:

Brianna! I've been praying for you and wondering how you were doing. Of course you can call. Any time, day or night. Questions are sacred things—they're how we grow. I'd be honored to wrestle with them alongside you.

She set the phone aside, feeling something she hadn't experienced in months: the sense that she was moving toward something instead of just running away. Not back to the faith of her childhood—that innocent certainty was gone forever, and she wouldn't want it back even if she could have it. But forward to something new, something big enough to hold both her questions and her tentative hope, her grief and her stubborn determination to keep loving despite the risk.

"Maya?" she said into the quiet of their room.

"Yeah?"

"I think I want to go to The Well this Sunday. Not to get saved or find all the answers. Just to... be with people who are brave enough to keep believing in something, even when it's complicated."

Maya set down her coffee cup, studying Brianna's face. "You know what? They'd love to have you. And complicated isn't the enemy—it's just... honest." Brianna traced the rim of her mug. "I spent so long thinking Liam had figured something out. That his whole 'nothing matters' thing was brave." She looked up. "But it wasn't bravery. It was just... safer." "Safer than what?" "Than admitting I wanted things to matter. Than risking disappointment." The words came slowly, like she was testing each one. "I thought if I could stop caring, stop hoping, then I couldn't get hurt. But I wasn't free—I was just... frozen."

Maya nodded, her expression gentle but not pitying. "And now?" "Now I'm terrified." Brianna's laugh was shaky. "But maybe that's the point? Maybe being scared means I'm actually alive again."

Outside their window, the campus settled into its late-night quiet—students tucked away in dorms and apartments, the small college town breathing slowly toward morning. Tomorrow there would be classes and the ordinary work of learning to live with questions that had no easy answers. But tonight, there was something like peace in having faced the void and chosen, however tentatively, to believe that emptiness wasn't the only truth. It wasn't the end of her questions or the resolution of her grief. But it was a beginning—the first steps toward a faith that could hold both doubt and hope, anger and love, the terrible reality of loss and the stubborn possibility of grace.

And in the growing quiet of Thursday becoming Friday, that felt like enough of a foundation to build on.

The morning after felt different—not triumphant, but clear. Brianna woke before her alarm to November sunlight streaming through their dorm window, pale but persistent, the kind of light that suggested winter was coming but hadn't arrived yet. She lay still for a moment, taking inventory of herself the way she'd learned to do after difficult nights. Her chest felt open instead of constricted. Her thoughts moved like water instead of grinding like gears.

The confrontation with Liam hadn't left her energized the way she'd expected. Instead, she felt something quieter—the bone-deep tiredness that came after carrying something heavy for a long time and finally being able to set it down.

Maya was already up, moving through her morning routine with the quiet efficiency of someone who'd learned to be considerate of roommates. She caught Brianna's eye in the mirror as she brushed her teeth and offered a small smile that asked *how are you?* without requiring words.

"Better," Brianna said, answering the unspoken question. "Weird, but better."

"Want to talk about it over coffee? The good stuff from that place downtown, not the brown water they serve in the dining hall."

Twenty minutes later, they were walking across campus in the crisp morning air, their breath visible in small puffs. The trees had finished their grand display of color, and were settling into the bare honesty of late autumn—branches stark against the sky, beautiful in their refusal to pretend they were anything other than what they were.

At Grounded, the coffee shop that had become their refuge from campus chaos, they found a corner table by the window. Maya ordered her usual lavender latte, while Brianna surprised herself by asking for something she hadn't had in months—a chai tea with extra cinnamon, sweet and warming, the kind of drink that tasted like comfort instead of defiance.

"So," Maya said, wrapping her hands around her mug, "do you want to tell me about last night? You looked like you'd seen a ghost when you came in."

"More like I'd finally stopped being one," Brianna said, then tried to explain the encounter with Liam—his casual cruelty disguised as wisdom, the girl hanging on his every word, the moment when she'd realized she was looking at her own recent past from the outside.

"He was so certain," she continued, staring into Maya's eyes. "Just like I used to be. About how the world works, about what people deserve."

Maya was quiet for a long moment, her fingers tracing the rim of her coffee cup. When she finally spoke, her voice carried the weight of something carefully preserved. "My aunt told me something once, right before she died. She'd lived through a war, lost everyone she'd ever loved, watched her whole world disappear." Maya paused, her throat working. "She said the greatest tragedy wasn't what happened to her—it was what she'd done to herself afterward. She said we build these magnificent fortresses to keep pain out, but we forget that the same walls that protect us from being shattered also protect us from being touched. From being changed. From being *alive*."

Maya's voice broke slightly. "She told me that every time we choose safety over connection, every time we choose cynicism over wonder, we die a little. That the people who hurt us—they don't just wound us in that moment. They convince us to keep wounding ourselves, day after day, year after year, until we become accomplices in our own disappearance." She looked directly at Brianna. "She said the most radical act of defiance isn't building higher walls—it's tearing them down. Again and again. Even when we know it will hurt. *Especially* then."

"But?" Maya prompted gently.

"But it wasn't relief. It was just... numbness. And numbness isn't the opposite of pain—it's the opposite of feeling anything at all. Including joy, or love, or the weird, complicated satisfaction of actually helping someone." She took a sip of her chai, the spices warm on her tongue. "I realized I didn't want to be right about the world being meaningless. I wanted to be wrong. I wanted there to be something worth believing in, even if believing meant risking being hurt again.

Maya nodded slowly. "That takes a different kind of courage than the kind Liam was selling."

"That's what scares me, though," Brianna admitted. "What if I'm just being naive again? What if the smart thing really is to expect nothing and feel nothing and protect myself from getting blindsided by loss?"

"Can I tell you something my aunt said to me, right before she died?" Maya's voice grew quiet, reverent. "I was so angry at the time, so convinced that God had failed us, that faith was just organized wishful thinking. And she looked at me with these eyes that were already halfway to somewhere else and said, 'Maya, honey, you can spend your whole life trying to protect yourself from being hurt, and you'll succeed. But you'll also succeed at protecting yourself from being loved, from being amazed, from being changed by the beautiful, terrible, necessary experience of being alive.'"

The words settled between them like a benediction. Outside the coffee shop window, students hurried past with backpacks and determination, their lives moving forward in ways that suddenly seemed miraculous instead of mundane—all those hearts beating, all those minds dreaming, all those people choosing to get up each day and engage with a world that offered no guarantees.

"I think," Brianna said slowly, "I'm ready to risk being hurt again. Not because I want to be, but because the alternative is too expensive. I can't afford to keep paying for my mother's death with my own life."

Maya reached across the table and squeezed her hand briefly—a gesture of solidarity, not pity. "What does that look like, practically?"

Brianna considered the question. "Calling my dad more often, even when I don't know what to say. Going to The Well on Sunday, even though I'm terrified I'll feel like a fraud. Maybe even..." She paused, the thought too new and fragile to examine too closely. "Maybe even praying again. Not the desperate bargaining kind I used to do, but something more like... showing up. Being honest about where I am instead of where I think I should be."

"God can work with honest," Maya said. "It's the pretending that makes things complicated."

They finished their coffee in comfortable silence, watching the world wake up around them. When they finally headed back to campus, Brianna felt something she hadn't experienced in months: anticipation for what might come next. Not the frantic hopefulness that had characterized her prayers during her mother's illness, but a quieter expectation—the sense that her story was still being written and that the next chapters might contain surprises that weren't exclusively devastating.

"Maya?" she said as they climbed the steps to their dorm.

"Yeah?"

"Thank you. For not giving up on me when I was determined to give up on myself. For leaving tea on my nightstand when I couldn't ask for help. For showing me what love looks like when it doesn't have an agenda."

Maya's smile was warm and uncomplicated. "Thank you for letting me. And for reminding me why faith is worth the risk, even when—especially when—it's hard."

Back in their room, Brianna pulled out her phone and did something that would have been unthinkable just twenty-four hours earlier. She called her father.

He picked up on the second ring, his voice cautious but hopeful. "Bree? Everything okay?"

"It's Brianna, Dad," she said, but gently this time, without the edge that had characterized their recent conversations. "And yes, everything's okay. I just... I wanted to talk. Are you free?"

"Always free for you, kiddo," he said, and she could hear him settling into his favorite chair, the old recliner that had been her mother's least favorite piece of furniture but that he couldn't bring himself to replace. "What's on your mind?"

"I've been thinking about Mom," she said, the words coming easier than she'd expected. "And about how angry I've been. At God, at the world, at you sometimes. I think I was angry at you for not falling apart the way I did, for going back to work and trying to keep things normal when normal felt like betrayal."

There was a long pause on the other end of the line. When her father spoke again, his voice was thick with emotion.

"Oh, honey. I wasn't keeping things now, he said quietly. "I thought you were handling it better than me. I thought maybe you didn't miss her as much as I did."

Her father's laugh was broken but genuine. "Baby girl, I miss her every single day. I wake up and for just a second, I forget she's gone. I reach for her side of the bed, or I start to call her name when something funny happens on TV. The grief counselor says that's normal, but it doesn't feel normal. It feels like my life is a song with all the harmonies missing."

They cried together over the phone—not the bitter, isolated tears Brianna had grown accustomed to, but the cleaner sadness that came from shared sorrow, from knowing you weren't carrying the weight alone.

"Dad?" she said eventually, when they'd both caught their breath.

"Yeah?"

"I love you. And I'm sorry I've been pushing you away. I was so afraid of .losing anyone else that I almost lost you too."

"You couldn't lose me if you tried," he said firmly. "I'm your dad. That's a lifetime contract, no matter how angry or scared or confused you get. We're going to figure this out together, okay? One day at a time."

After they hung up, Brianna sat in the quiet of her room and marveled at how different silence could feel when it wasn't born of isolation. This was the silence of peace, of having said true things and been heard, of having offered love and had it received.

Sunday was three days away, and with it, her first return to anything resembling corporate worship since her mother's funeral. The thought still made her stomach flutter with anxiety, but it was a different kind of nervousness than she'd felt before. Not the fear of being judged or found wanting, but the natural apprehension that came before any meaningful risk.

She was going to show up with her questions intact, her anger unresolved, her faith tentative and fragile as new growth. She was going to risk believing in something bigger than her own pain, not because she was certain it would work out, but because she was finally ready to find out what happened when you choose hope over self-protection.

It felt terrifying and necessary and strangely like coming home to a place she'd never been before.

Outside their window, the November afternoon was settling into evening, the light growing golden and slanted in the way that made ordinary things look sacred. Brianna pulled out a notebook and began to write—not the angry, defensive essays she'd crafted for months, but something different. A letter to her mother, maybe, or to God, or to the version of herself that was brave enough to believe that love was stronger than loss, that meaning could be found in the midst of suffering, that grace was real even when it came wearing the face of a roommate with chamomile tea instead of the angels she'd been expecting.

The words came slowly at first, then faster, as if they'd been waiting for permission to exist. And in the writing, in the choosing to hope instead of despair, in the decision to reach toward light instead of retreating into comfortable darkness, Brianna felt something she'd almost forgotten existed: the quiet joy of being fully alive in a complicated world, of being brave enough to love it anyway.

Letter to Mom

October 15th, 2:30 AM

Mom,

I'm writing this at the kitchen table where we used to sit when I couldn't sleep. Remember how you'd make that terrible chamomile tea that tasted like grass, and we'd talk about everything and nothing? I could use some of that terrible tea right now.

I keep thinking about what you said near the end – about seeds. How some truths have to be planted in the dark before they can grow. I was so angry then, watching you fade away while still trying to teach me things. I wanted you to fight harder, not give me garden metaphors. But maybe that's exactly what you were doing – fighting for me in the only way you had left.

My roommate, Maya, who reminds me of you sometimes. Not in looks, but in the way she sees people. She makes me feel like I matter, like my questions aren't character flaws that need fixing. And there's Dr. Finch – I know you'd like him. He doesn't try to wrap pain in pretty bows. He just sits with it, helps you find the shape of it.

I'm learning that I don't have to have everything figured out to keep moving forward. That maybe wisdom isn't about having all the right answers, but about asking better questions. Like why did I spend so long running from every good thing you tried to give me? And how did you manage to plant hope in me even when you were losing yours?

I still get angry sometimes. At the cancer, at God, at you for leaving me to figure this out alone. But I'm starting to understand that love doesn't disappear just because bodies do. The way you saw the world, the way you loved people despite their brokenness – that's still here. Growing in me, even in the dark places.

I miss your voice, your laugh, the way you'd hum while doing dishes. I miss feeling like someone understood me completely. But those seeds you planted? They're starting to sprout, Mom. Finally.

Love you, Brianna

Letter to God

Written in the margins of my journal

God,

I don't even know if you're real, but I'm writing this anyway because Dr. Finch says questions can be prayers too. If that's true, then I've been praying non-stop for months, just not the kind they taught me in Sunday school.

I'm angry at you. There, I said it. I'm furious that you took my mom, that you let people like Liam twist faith into something ugly and manipulative, that you stay silent when I scream into the void at 3 AM. If you exist, your customer service sucks.

But here's the thing I'm struggling with – despite everything, I can't shake the feeling that there's something more. Not the neat, packaged version I grew up with, where good people get blessed and bad people get punished. That's obviously garbage. But something bigger than me, something that moves through Maya's kindness and Dr. Finch's wisdom and the way strangers sometimes show up exactly when you need them.

Liam said faith was about certainty, about having all the right beliefs lined up like trophies on a shelf. He made it sound like doubt was failure, like questions were weakness. But what if it's the opposite? What if real faith is more like learning to dance with uncertainty, to find God in the struggle instead of in the answers?

I don't know how to pray anymore, at least not the way I used to. The words feel foreign now, too small for what I'm carrying. But maybe that's okay. Maybe prayer isn't about pretty words or proper theology. Maybe it's just this – showing up honestly, bringing all my mess and doubt and hope to whatever might be listening.

If you're real, help me understand the difference between faith and pretending. Help me find you in the questions, not just in the answers. And if

I'm just talking to myself, well, at least I'm finally being honest about what I'm actually thinking.

   Still searching, Brianna

Letter to Past Me

Found in my old Bible

Dear Sixteen-Year-Old Brianna,

You're going to run. I know that now, and I understand why. The church feels suffocating, full of people who have neat answers for messy questions. You're going to sit in that youth group listening to them explain away your mom's cancer like it's part of some divine plan, and something inside you is going to break. You'll walk out, and you won't come back.

That's okay. You need to run. Your heart is so raw, so full of rage and questions that have no good answers. The people around you mean well, but they're scared of your pain. They want to fix you, to smooth your sharp edges into something more comfortable. But you don't need fixing – you need space to grieve, to rage, to figure out who you are when everything you believed gets torn apart.

You're going to make some mistakes. You'll meet someone named Liam who will use your questions against you, who will make cynicism feel like sophistication. You'll think that rejecting faith means rejecting the possibility of hope entirely. But that's just another kind of cage, sweetheart. Don't let your hurt harden into something that can't bend.

Here's what I wish I could tell you: your questions aren't dangerous. Your doubt isn't failure. The fact that you can't make peace with easy answers isn't a character flaw – it's integrity. You're looking for something real, something that can hold all of who you are, including the parts that are angry and broken and scared.

You're going to find people who get this. Maya, who will show you that community doesn't have to mean conformity. Dr. Finch, who will teach you that wisdom looks more like curiosity than certainty. They'll help you understand that coming home doesn't mean going backward.

The seeds Mom planted in you? They're still there, even when you can't feel them growing. Trust the process, even when it feels like wandering. Especially then.

With love and understanding, Future You

P.S. – Keep writing. The questions you're asking now will become the prayers that save you later.

Discussion Questions for "Running from Sunday"

General Themes & Character Development:

1. Brianna starts the book believing the key to surviving college is to "need absolutely nothing from anyone." How does this philosophy manifest in her early interactions, and how does it evolve throughout the story?

2. The metaphor of the "fortress" is central to Brianna's journey. How does she build her initial fortress, what does it protect her from, and what are its ultimate limitations? How is this echoed in Liam's own "fortress"?

3. Maya's character provides a stark contrast to Brianna's initial approach to grief. How does Maya's personal experience with loss shape her own "relentless optimism" and "careful kindness"? What makes her different from the "comforting platitudes" Brianna despises?

4. Liam is introduced as an "antidote" to the "bull" Brianna finds everywhere. Initially, what makes his perspective so appealing to

her? How does her perception of him and his "Gospel of Nothing" change over time?

5. Dr. Finch plays a significant role in challenging Brianna's worldview. What specific insights or actions from Dr. Finch are most impactful for Brianna, and why?

6. The story explores different kinds of "faith" – from the childhood certainty Brianna once held, to Liam's "Gospel of Nothing," to Maya and Dr. Finch's more nuanced understandings. How are these different forms of faith (or lack thereof) presented, and what are their respective strengths and weaknesses?

7. How does Brianna's relationship with her father evolve throughout the story? What is the significance of their phone calls, particularly in later chapters?

8. The concept of "anger" is explored extensively. How does Brianna initially use anger, and how does her understanding of it transform? What does it mean for anger to be "the most honest prayer you can offer"?

9. By the end of the chapters, Brianna is in a "threshold between the past and the future." What does this mean for her, and what does the story suggest about the nature of healing or growth?

Specific Chapter Focus:

Chapter 1: Discuss the opening scene where Brianna and Maya first meet. What immediate impressions do you get of each character, and how do their opposing approaches to their dorm room symbolize their differing coping mechanisms?

Chapter 2: What is the significance of the cross necklace for Brianna? How does Liam navigate her discomfort with religious topics, and what does their initial connection feel like for Brianna?

Chapter 3: Compare and contrast the different invitations Brianna receives for her first Friday night (The Well vs. the fraternity party). What do these choices represent for her at this stage of her grief? How does Maya's quiet observation of Brianna's decision impact the scene?

Chapter 4: The Sunday morning ghost. How does the memory of her mother's Sundays impact Brianna's day? What role does Maya's personal revelation about her aunt's death play in beginning to shift Brianna's perspective?

Chapter 5: Discuss Brianna's essay on Hopkins. What is she *really* arguing against, and what does it reveal about her own internal state? How does Dr. Finch's response challenge her in unexpected ways?

Chapter 6: Liam introduces Brianna to the "Gospel of Nothing." How does this concept resonate with her initial grief, and what makes it feel like "salvation" to her? How do his words both relieve and subtly entrap her?

Chapter 7 & 8: The sequence involving Maya's cup of tea and Brianna's later confrontation with Liam is pivotal. How does this singular act of kindness begin to dismantle Brianna's hardened worldview? What does she realize about Liam's philosophy during their coffee shop conversation?

Chapter 9: The memory of her mother's advice about faith and doubt is crucial. How does this memory provide a new lens for Brianna to understand her own experiences and choices? What is the significance of her mother's "planting seeds" metaphor?

Chapter 10 & 11: Trace Brianna's "small, tentative steps" towards healing. What specific changes in her behavior and outlook indicate this shift?

How do the conversations with Dr. Finch and Maya about "wrestling with faith" provide her with permission and a new framework?

Chapter 12 (Epilogue letters): Discuss the three letters Brianna writes. What does each letter reveal about her current understanding of her past, her present, and her potential future? What is the significance of her "Letter to Past Me" and its advice about courage and truth?

Symbolism and Imagery:

1. Identify recurring symbols or images (e.g., fairy lights, gray/black vs. color, the fortress, scaffolding, seeds/gardening, coffee/tea). What do these symbols represent, and how do they underscore the story's themes?

2. How is "silence" used throughout the story? What different meanings does it take on for Brianna (e.g., God's silence, the silence of grief, the peaceful quiet)?

Personal Reflection:

1. Has Brianna's journey resonated with your own experiences of grief, doubt, or questioning deeply held beliefs?

2. What character do you relate to most: Brianna, Maya, Liam, or Dr. Finch? Why?

3. The story suggests that "real faith... has to be big enough to hold questions." What does this mean to you? How do you think healing from trauma or loss impacts one's spiritual or philosophical beliefs?

About the author

I've spent over four decades watching and participating in the digital revolution. From my first encounters with computer programming in high school during the late 1970s to navigating today's complex cyber landscape, technology has been a constant companion in my journey. While serving in the U.S. Army during Desert Storm, I witnessed firsthand how rapidly technology could evolve and transform our capabilities.

Now, as I navigate my senior years, I find myself in a unique position – someone who understands both the tremendous potential and the growing challenges of our digital age. This book represents not just my knowledge, but our shared experience as we continue to adapt and learn in this ever-changing digital world.

Through her writing, Rene' aims to illuminate the positive aspects of life's journey, drawing from her varied experiences to create stories that resonate with readers of all backgrounds.

Readers can discover more about Rene's work at www.books-by-rene.store